BORDER
CROSSINGS

BORDER CROSSINGS

A NOVEL BY JOHN FAIRWEATHER

SUNSTONE
PRESS

SANTA FE
NEW MEXICO

All characters, incidents, and dialogue in this book are the products of the authors imagination and are not to be construed as real. Depictions are fictional and any resemblance to actual events or persons, living or dead, is therefore entirely coincidental.

Library of Congress Cataloging in Publication Data:
Fairweather, John, 1951-
    Border crossings: a novel / by John Fairweather.
      P. cm.
    ISBN: 0-86534-002-1: $14.95
    I. Title.
PS3556.A3655B67   1995
813' .54—dc20   94-43832
                  CIP

Published by   SUNSTONE PRESS
               Post Office Box 2321
               Santa Fe, NM 87504-2321 / USA
               (505) 988-4418 / *orders only* (800) 243-5644
               FAX (505) 988-1025

Cover design and illustration by Beth Evans

To
Tom, my friend,
still crossing borders;
and
Beth, my wife,
who helped me across this one.

Special thanks to Sylvia, who sacrificed her teacher's Spring Break to help; Don, who convinced me experience was the best way; Teresa and Teri who typed this and still like me; Glen, the unknown poet of the final chapter; Jim, my editor who edits as slim as Barbie's waist; and my students Tim and Lauren, who contributed their mature insight. Never doubt the new generation. They aren't so different from us.

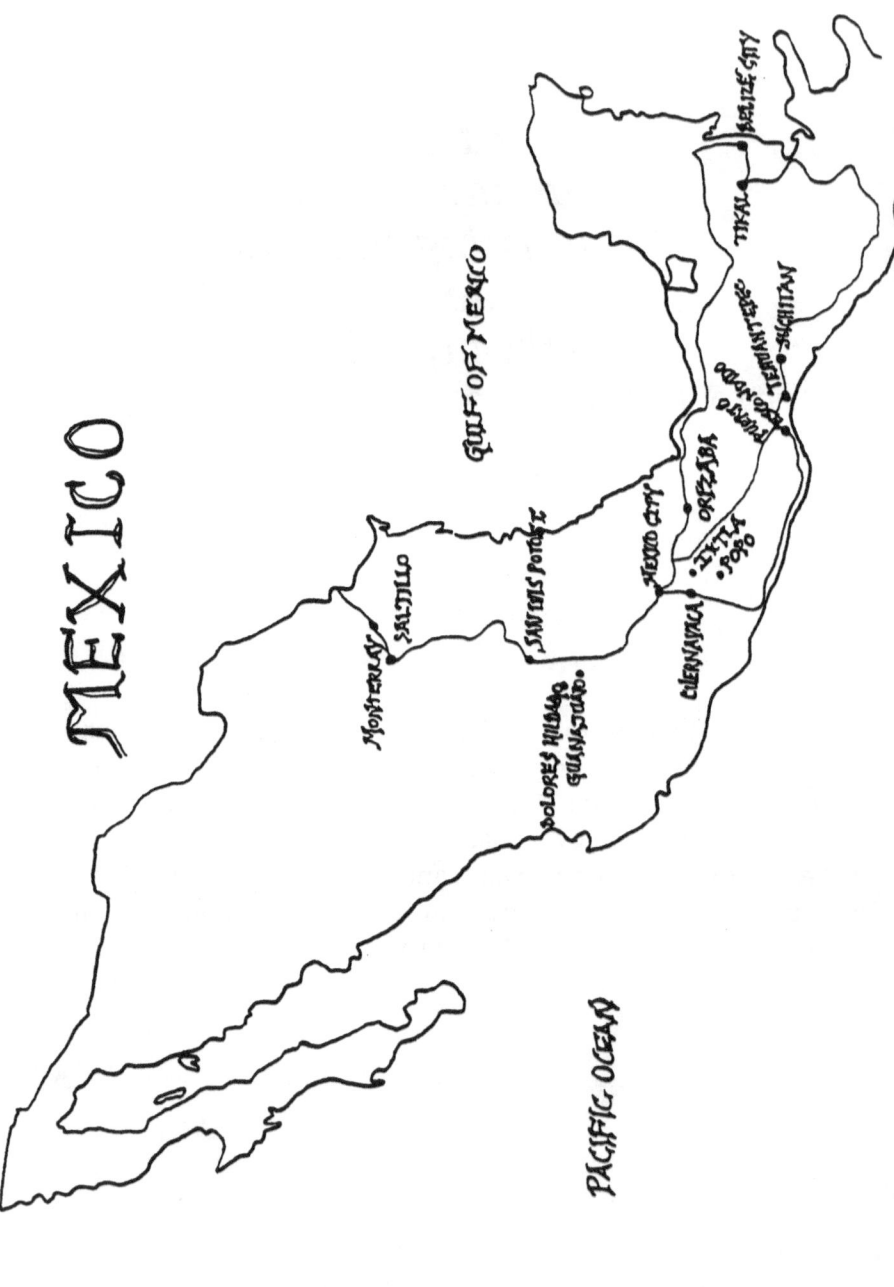

MEXICO

GULF OF MEXICO

PACIFIC OCEAN

Monterrey
Saltillo
San Luis Potosi
Dolores Hidalgo
Guanajuato
Mexico City
Cuernavaca
Yautla
Orizaba
Puebla
Puerto Nuevo
Coatzacoalcos
Villahermosa
Palenque
Tikal
Belize City

PRELUDE

"Entering Mexico is relatively simple: all that is needed is proof
of citizenship and a tourist card."

—AAA Road Atlas

I crossed the border at Laredo on August 10, 1974, leaving
behind a dead father and a worried mother, an acceptance to
the University of Alabama Law School, an obsessive interest in
the Civil War, a 1-H draft classification and an unfaithful fiance who
deserted me for a one hundred sixty-five pound wrestler who put
together model airplanes.

I would miss my mother. She would be lonely for a while. After
eight years of battling lung cancer, my father had died on December
4, 1972, one day before his sixty-eighth birthday. He had taken all
the radiation treatments possible, burning out both the cancer cells
and the healthy ones, until his body shrank and turned as pink as
the inside of a sea shell, and his eyes glowed bloodshot. But he
persisted, feeling, I guess, that he must be destroyed to live.

On the day of his last trip to the hospital, he was so weak I had
to shave him, his face so drawn he had to press his tongue against
the inside of his cheeks so the razor could reach his beard. While
I shaved, he insisted on watching the Alabama-Auburn Southeast-
ern Conference championship football game on television in the
den. He cheered while Bear Bryant, invincible as stone, prowled the
sidelines. Alabama won the game thirty-one to six.

My mother, hoping my father's battle would soon be over,
twiddled her hands nervously in the kitchen. They had been married
twenty-five years, but she didn't want him to face the truth. Her

mission was care, comfort and waiting. There would be friends, prayers and casseroles, and then her new life would begin.

When the ambulance and the stretcher bearers came, he waved goodbye, calling weakly, "I'll be back." Truthfully, I didn't miss him then, and I didn't for quite a while. I knew his death would make things easier for us. I tried. I put on a long face and moped around for a few weeks, but it was all a show.

I wouldn't miss the law school. I sweated through four dusty years as a student assistant filing documents in its dim library stacks and had developed a hatred for the claustrophobic smell of dead paper filled with the dark words of impersonal forces. And I learned I didn't want to become a lawyer, especially one that dealt with personal injury. However, I had learned to do this boring job quickly, and spent many hours reading my own documents about the Civil War and the struggles of the Twentieth Alabama Infantry.

Sergeant David Bragg, my favorite ancestor and my family's only hero, had served with General E.W. Pettus' brigade of the Twentieth Alabama from Vicksburg to Nashville. He was shot in the chest covering the retreat from the Harpeth river, where according to General Clayton's official report of the battle, "Pettus' brigade, supported by the Thirty-ninth Georgia, were in line at Nashville after all the rest of the army was in 'entire route.'"

Earlier in the war, during the battles on Lookout Mountain and Missionary Ridge, Pettus' brigade also was commended. General Stevenson stated in his report of the battle on November 27, 1864, that "It was Pettus' brigade (David Bragg's unit) which first checked an enemy flushed with victory on Lookout Mountain, and held him at bay until forced to retire." And about the next day's battle on Missionary Ridge, General E.W. Pettus himself wrote that "the Twentieth Alabama behaved gallantly."

They may have behaved gallantly, but it bothered me that they usually seemed to be covering retreats by fighting heroically so that others could escape. Shouldn't they have been charging with Celtic nostrils flaring and voices screaming the rebel yell into the rifle pits of the enemy? Or was there honor in a well-fought, orderly retreat?

After the battle at Nashville, the gallant David Bragg's father had rescued him from a field hospital and driven him back to the Braggville family home in the single family wagon. The rest had been confiscated by the Confederate Army.

David Bragg lived to sign the Oath of Allegiance required of Ex-Confederate soldiers after the surrender. In scrawling brown ink it read:

I, David Bragg, hereby swear allegiance to the Constitution of the United States of America, and agree hereafter to abide by its laws and statutes.

I didn't like the ending, the surrender. I felt he could have won a personal victory by refusing to sign that oath, because after the signing he had little to look forward to but a predictable life and a lingering death. Gasping for air, he died in 1899 of pneumonia caused by the Springfield rifle slug in his left lung.

I had missed my chance to be the next family hero when I missed Vietnam. I missed the draft lottery by two numbers (I was 128 and they took only up to 126), and I didn't volunteer. Despite my love of the Civil War, I was afraid. I couldn't translate my own personal documents into action, instead, I lived them through the pictures in my imagination and escaped reality by avoiding the six o'clock news. It was the face of Walter Cronkite and not the face of George Pickett before his charge at Gettysburg that dominated my historical vision. I played peek-a-boo with peanut butter sandwiches and the sports' pages and turned the volume down real low.

I wasn't afraid of death, its instant and beyond, rather I was afraid of losing life and its time stretch of events. Besides, by 1974, the days of heros in that war had long been over. We were in retreat. It was only a year away, our forgotten Vietnamese disciples waving their arms helplessly towards the packed, departing helicopters.

The scripture of that war was written not by the Official War Records, but by the Rolling Stones who told us that *"we couldn't get no satisfaction."* But I was not in that war and I had satisfaction, at least for while.

But I lost it.

I would miss Evelyn, my fiance. She had been the satisfaction that was gone. I couldn't have left her for gold, glory or God, as the old Spanish Conquistadors used to say, because like their obsessions, she had become mine, guts and soul. I was hypocritical, searching for the same strength in surrender that I thought my ancestor had sought.

What I remember most about our time together is the blush of her butt, summer tan lines still faintly visible, warming over the gas heater in my rented house. It was an overseer's old place, secluded down a gravel road and only fifty yards from the GMN&O railroad tressels, the longest remaining wooden one in the United States. On cool fall nights I loved to hear the eleven o'clock trains grating wheels while we made love in my spooled bed that had belonged to a Confederate colonel. The Black Warrior river smacked its cool lips nearly to our doorstep, and in the warmth of thick patch quilts, I felt the solitude of two and knew that Crosby, Stills and Nash were right when they sang to us that

> *Our bodies were a perfect fit,*
> *In afterglow we lay,*
> *My lady of the Isle.*

Evelyn and I were born on the same day, December 28, 1951, and we both majored in history and minored in English. I was heading towards law school and she was already working on her M.A. in educational administration. Our life together seemed to have direction, the clock hands moving smoothly in measured minutes and away from the angst that had infected so many of our generation. I thought we were free.

But thirty-three days after we became engaged, I found her in her dorm room bed with the college wrestler, an athlete with muscles chiseled like Michelangelo's David. It was deliberate: she had timed me to find her. The David was cupping her right breast with both hands and sucking it as savagely as a hungry baby. When she saw me, she didn't even stop him. Without blinking, she just looked into my startled eyes. I left. I watched the Julia Tutwilder dormitory door until eleven o'clock that night when the David left. Then I called my love from a pay phone at the corner drug store.

"Why," I asked.

"I tried to tell you but you wouldn't listen," she said.

"What, what did you try to tell me?"

"That you didn't give me any space, my own room."

"But did you have to do it that way?" I moaned, breaking into tears.

"It was the only way. It was the only way I could escape." Despite the passing cars, there was a stillness in the booth, and the light from the street burst through the scratched plastic like exploding stars.

For ten minutes after she hung up, I listened to the phone drone its apathetic whir. Then I ran to the old Confederate ruins by the Amelia Gayle Gorgas Library and screamed like a two-year old until the campus police came.

My life was a sinkhole. I thought I needed a new personal history and new myths. I quit my job, broke my lease, cleaned out my savings, kissed my mother goodbye and lit out for Mexico in my new Capri.

I wouldn't miss my music because it was with me, in my head, my heart, and my eight-track tape player. Mainly, I took the music of the late sixties. These songs were the benchmarks of my life, spanning childhood fantasies to teenage realities, and creating temporarily, an invisible emotional world of escape. I hadn't had a social or political philosophy during the sixties, or even during my college years in the early seventies, rather I had a personal one, and the lyrics of that time were its expression, its poetry.

I traveled Interstate 10 across the bowels of Mississippi and Louisiana, lands so raped by the lumber companies that the only vegetation left was skinny pine trees sticking up like lint-covered toothpicks. I crossed the oil lands of Texas past wells jutting from the plains like penises strung together with chicken wire from the hard, waist-flat plains. In San Antonio I switched to Interstate 35, blew past the Alamo and headed across Texas cattle country towards Laredo and the Rio Grande.

I was on my way to a teaching job with Mexico City's private school for the diplomats' kids, The American School Foundation. I had gotten this job through the career planning office at the university. Its prospectus stated that its purpose was to "provide an American curricula with instruction in American values. Its merits were that "60% of our students attend distinguished American universities including Harvard, Yale, Duke, and Michigan." Decorating the front page was the school's coat of arms, the flags of the United States and Mexico crossed like sabers during a military ceremony.

Across the border, in Nuevo Laredo, I was supposed to meet Tom, my future roommate. Tom was an art teacher and sculptor who had already spent a year working at the American School. Career planning had put me in touch with him as a possible roommate and companion. We met in Tuscaloosa briefly and discovered we shared a fondness for beer, sorority girls (Evelyn was a Zeta) and lies. Tom bragged about how much he had enjoyed getting his bachelor's degree after seven hard years of work. His education had been interrupted by travel. After having been partially paralyzed in a car accident in 1967, he won a hefty lawsuit and spent it bumming around Europe for a year and living with the fading hippie culture in San Francisco until 1970, when it turned ugly as mud. Then he returned to Alabama and finished his degree before ending up in Mexico by the same route I did.

After miles of emptiness, I approached Laredo and the border. I was hoping to fill the spaces within myself and seek meaning through adventures, new women and the living history of long dead gods. I didn't know that this search would take me over the crags of evil and across the high deserts of despair. I didn't suspect that the vials of emptiness also waited in Mexico, waited to be filled with the poisons of self-delusion. And I didn't know how difficult it would be to escape this old part of the New World. I only knew I was leaving behind the life-Americana, planned like pasteurized milk from the grass to the glass.

From my eight-track Bob Dylan's raspy, prophetic voice sang

> *There must be some way out of here,*
> *Said the joker to the thief.*
> *There's too much confusion;*
> *I can't get no relief.*
> *Outside in the distance,*
> *A wildcat did growl.*
> *Two riders were approaching,*
> *And the wind began to howl.*

1

We'll meet on edges soon, said I
Proud 'neath heated brow.
Ah, but I was so much younger then,
I'm younger then than now.

— Bob Dylan

At Laredo, I crossed the bridge and Laredo became Nuevo Laredo, Interstate 35 became Highway 85 and the Rio Grande became the Rio Bravo. Within minutes, I had shown my FM 3 working papers and passport, cleared customs (I had nothing but some clothes and a box of books) and was on Guerrero Avenue in the heart of town. It was easier than I had imagined.

I checked into the Ramada Inn where I was supposed to meet Tom the next day, and then drove to the Departamento de Automobiles where my car papers would be processed. All foreign residents working or studying in Mexico were required to register their cars and pay a fee. This was supposed to keep the sneaky capitalist from driving quality American cars to Mexico and selling them for exorbitant profits.

The Departamento de Automobiles was located on a seedy side street that smelled of piss and greasy food. Like a mocking sidewalk surfer, a legless beggar seated on a homemade skateboard scooted around the entrance. I gave him a dollar. A middle-aged American tourist tried to give him another to take his picture, but the beggar rolled around the corner quickly by pushing himself along with his arms. The tourist followed yelling, "Hey wait, I'll give you more."

The building itself was a city-block large warehouse with a corrugated tin roof that heated up the inside like a waffle iron. There was no air conditioning, only a small fan aimed at the government official whose job was to process the paperwork of the dozens of people crowded before his desk. He typed these paper mountains with two slow fingers. Peck-Peck-Peck-Peck. And he stopped often. The order of service was random and he made no effort to change this procedure despite exasperated complaints from the sweaty mob. Every now and then he looked up, removed the papers from the manual typewriter, and declared in perfect English, "Mr. Mercedes 1973, your papers are ready. Please pay two thousand dollars in cash for your fees. Sign here. And here. And you cannot leave the country without your car. Thank you."

After several hours in the dirty, asphyxiating heat, a man with a cadillac cried for mercy and speed. He pushed his way to the desk and shoved an envelope at the official. He took it, placed it in a drawer and continued typing. Mr. Michael retreated to the back of the warehouse for air. He was still there at the end of the day, poorer for his practical efforts. Since I was entertained watching many such demands for order, my own wait wasn't so bad. After all, it was the predictable daily grind I was trying to escape.

After two days of waiting I still didn't have my car papers and Tom still hadn't arrived. Despite the human interest fascination in the warehouse, I needed a break from its heat, so I decided to get some fresh air and visit a small carnival I'd heard about a few miles out of the city on Highway 85. I had expected the wholesome county fairs of the South with dizzy rides, cotton candy at the Elks booth, teddy bear games, a lively girley show and everyone's star attraction, the freak show. I found all of this, but this carnival had a real freak show, a much crueler one. American shows consist mainly of cheap actors and frauds impersonating alligator men and mermaids. Their purpose: to intrigue the spectators and make them marvel. But in this south of the border freak show, babies with three arms and no faces glared at me from inside clear gallon jars filled with fluid; animals, alive still, with hideous and painful deformities, wailed their misfortunes; five-dollar prostitutes, their thin, crooked fingers extended from tent flaps, motioned for customers; and toothless midgets, the main attraction for the plebeian sportsman, fought boxing matches until they dropped from exhaustion or injury. I felt like a visitor to an undiscovered circle of hell, a purgatorial waiting room for the rational.

The punching midgets didn't have the luxury of a tent. Instead, they fought in an open pit while the fans, craning their necks like curious roosters, vied for a spot around the perimeter. They sat in their respective corners, watching for the fat young girl standing with a cow bell in the center of the pit to gong the contest's first round. One midget was dressed in a cowboy suit complete with chaps, boots and hat. The other wore Indian garb, feather headdress, war paint and all. Their faces were already purple and swollen from previous fights and the cowboy's lip looked sewn from its edge, giving him another smile that zigzagged, sketching on him another, more menacing identity.

The bell clanged and the midgets clashed with a flurry of punches. The blows thudded, sounding like someone striking a pillow in anger. The crowd shouted encouragement at their favorites, money changing hands continuously. They moved like old family friends shaking hands at a reunion. I remembered I had read about slave fights before the emancipation. The owners picked the strongest racehorse-muscular negroes to square off against one another, fighting in the nude. I wondered how the slaves felt to face each other without rancor and not for money, but only for the gamblers' satisfaction. But at least they were a contest of the strong, not the weak, and there were no costumes in those arenas of naked gain.

The fight lasted three rounds of irregular length. Between rounds, the fat girl, who was dressed in a short, revealing black lace outfit, strutted like a hen to the center of the pit and held up a sign advertising Corona beer. Some men threw pesos at her. She bent over and retrieved them, being careful to spread her crack. After round two, both fighters had bleeding noses and the Indian's feathers were crushed. This was obviously an anything goes fight because the cowboy kept kicking the Indian with his pointed boots and the Indian seized the cowboy's head and bit a chunk out of his ear. Finally, after about a ten minute third round, the cowboy collapsed in a heap from several blows delivered to the top of his head. Good naturedly, with slaps on the back and laughter, the losers paid. Leaving the pit, I saw the fat girl holding up a sign advertising another fight that night.

I returned to the Ramada Inn and tried to get drunk but couldn't, gave up and tried to sleep but was kept awake by a feeling of dull terror, as if I had just awakened from a childhood nightmare in which I could not scream.

On the third morning, my papers were ready. I stepped out of the warehouse and into the sunlight and the familiar sounds of The Who

>...Keep me movin, over fifty,
>Just a hippie gypsy...
>Watch the po-lice and the taxman miss me
>I'm mobile...

Across the street was Tom's Chevy van, all doors open, blaring that freedom message. Like a tropical bird on display in a pet store, Tom sat cross-legged on his van carpet, his shoulder-length brown hair draped over the back of his tee shirt which read, *A Woman's Place Is On Top*. His clean, faded jeans were ripped across the knee and he was bare footed. A thick mustache rode across his upper lip, partially concealing his uneven teeth and imitating a cartoon villain. "Hey Bro," he greeted me through the foam of a Tecate beer. "What took ya so long to find me? That Ramada Inn greaser told me you'd been here three days. I got here last night, spent the night in the van, laid a rich senorita and got my van papers early this morning."

"How did you cut through this mess so fast?"

"I don't know," Tom laughed. "Maybe ole speedy in there is a maricon, you know that's Mexican for queer. Maybe he liked my looks as much as that senorita did last night. She was coming back from one of those rich shopping trips to Houston. I guess I was her first American present. We met at the Ramada Inn while I was waiting for you to show up. The bartender said that you had just left when I got there. You should have waited, something would have come along."

"What's the plan now?" I was anxious to get started.

"Plan? No plans. Just a little advice. Stay behind me down the road to Mexico City. But watch out for the Mexican truck drivers coming from the other direction. They pass in the middle of the road by creating three lanes where there are only two. Don't panic, they know what they're doing. Just pray they're not drunk. It's almost a straight shot to Mexico D.F. Let's get going."

2

Highway 85 took us across the high Mexican desert. The only escape from it was north, towards Laredo and the United States of America. The August afternoon heat seared the terrain and the landscape undulated like a dirty bedsheet flapping on a clothesline during a dust storm. Ragged Mexican children appeared out of the haze like characters on a slow-warming television screen. They stood on the arrow-straight highway holding small iguanas by their tails, hoping to sell them to a startled tourist. They reminded me of miniature dinosaurs that I feared would someday rise out of my nightmares to devour me, gulping my terrors into their waiting stomachs.

I left the creatures fading in the dust and followed Tom toward Monterray, just 989 miles from Mexico City. He had picked up a hitchhiker, an old Mexican peasant, and I could see the old man gesturing frantically with one arm as Tom drove, the old man's sombrero nodding sporadically in agreement. Mexicans always seemed to understand Tom, despite his poor Spanish that never improved. They understood him because he spoke the primitive language of pantomime. He spoke a few Spanish nouns and accented the only verb tense he knew, the present. This energetic form of expression endeared Tom to the Mexicans because most of them were forced to live life the way of Tom's language, in the present. I noticed that they agreed, or appeared to agree, with most of Tom's conversation, nodding vigorously as his hands picked up speed and attempted communication through motion. Even though I spoke more Spanish, it was Tom who was always more effective because he appealed to their imaginations while I struggled for their rationality.

I drank my tenth Bohemia and watched the coming mountains change from purple to fiery red and then disappear into the night shadows. Soon we were engulfed by the industrial waste pit of Monterry. This wasn't the Mexico I had heard about, read about and dreamed about. It looked like Birmingham, the smokestacks handing out their calling cards to cancer. Drunk and hungry, I followed Tom into the campground at the southern bottom of town. The peasant slid down from the van's front seat, refused a sandwich from Tom, said a short "gracious" and slipped like a spirit into Monterrey's darkness.

That night in the Monterrey campground, Tom took on another hitchhiker, a Scarlet Macaw named Carlota. The owner, a New York couple in a Volkswagen van, were moving back to the States and didn't want any problems with customs. They wanted fifty dollars, but Tom got her for free after he told them several horror stories. She would become Tom's master. It was six months before Tom could touch her and she never allowed the affection of any other male, especially me. Like an ancient Mexican god, she demanded sacrifice and loyalty and gave nothing in return.

We left at dawn to take advantage of the morning cool. Outside Saltillo, before we entered the mountains, we stopped for breakfast at a small restaurant, a parado, which was only a concrete hut with an open, thatched roof and dirt floor eating area. It was surrounded by a broken rail fence that pigs and goats entered freely. Inside, there were tin card tables with Coco-Cola and Carte Blanc painted over their rusty white tops. A soft-drink cooler containing beer and cold drinks occupied one corner. A spigot dripping water was in another. Three Mexican blue-collar workers in khaki pants and caps drank coffee at the table closest to the cooler. At another table, a dark Mexican girl about eighteen sat reading a pulp novel titled "Los Romanticos." On its cover a blond girl with terrified blue eyes struggled to liberate herself from the passionately violent grasp of her male seducer. Tom and I sat down by the reader's table.

"See that senorita with tits like cantaloupes," Tom pointed. "You're her grinning Nordic God, like that hero on the book's cover. Look at her. You can read that book by watching."

I watched. Her silent world became visible: brown eyes widened, the corners of her mouth curled upward revealing gold trimmed teeth, she fingered her wiry black hair, her thighs moved in and out expectantly.

"Oye, senorita," Tom called. "Es una novela romantica?" Her eyes squinted at us, she slammed her thighs together, and protective hands quickly cradled the novel. She suddenly pushed out her chair and walked quickly, glancing with fierce eyes over her shoulder, out of the parado and toward the bus stop down the road. The pesos for her bill were already on the table.

Three workers quit talking and gave Tom a cold iron stare. "Just ignore them," Tom advised. "They don't like Americans messing with their women. Playing with girls of her kind is like trying to hustle the wrong waitress at the Star Truck Stop on Highway 82. You know, the good ole boys want to beat your ass for messing with their woman, even if she isn't."

We ordered juevos rancheros and tortillas. "Now this is a

restaurant, Bro," Tom said, taking a deep pull of fresh orange juice. "None of that plastic motel food here. You'll get a little sweat in your eggs, gives them a little personality, like Black Bar-B-Q in Alabama. But Bro, you're going to have to be careful when you order juevos here in Mexico. You see, to a senorita eggs mean the same thing as balls. You can have some fun with it though if you know when to use it."

"Don't these girls get insulted? I saw how successful you were with the last one."

"It's a game, Bro. They love it, especially the peasant girls. You're their phantom conqueror, their conquistador. They love to lose, except for the whores. They always win, always have. But it's not worth it sometimes. These Indian girls have real flat asses, like ironing boards and they bite a lot. One hun in Mexico City put a hole in my lip and left tooth marks on my pecker." Tom pointed out a small scar hidden under his moustache. "And they don't know shit about birth control and they don't care, they're Catholic you know, so you've got to be careful. If you get one pregnant, it's a free lifelong trip to Disneyland if she lets the authorities know. If you lay one, don't speak Spanish, don't give your real name and get the hell away from her as quickly as possible, Comprende?"

"Doesn't sound very safe, professor. Maybe I'll be celibate, more of a friar than a conquistador."

"No, Bro. That's not the way. Give them a chance to live out their fantasies. That's the fun of it."

We continued on Highway 57 towards San Luis Potasi, surviving the kama-kazi transfer trucks spinning around the steep curves. There were international signs warning of falling rocks and I wondered where I would go if one came my way. In my sweaty solace, I slammed Fleetwood Mac into my tape player:

> There's a place down in Mexico,
> Where men can fly over mountains....

3

S outh of San Luis Potasi we crossed the Rio Santa Maria and entered the old colonial province of Guanajuato. This was silver country. Cortez had learned about the mines by studying Montezuma's tribute records. In these highlands, the early Spanish settlers had killed thousands of Indians and Mestizos when they forced that human chattel to climb out of deep holes carrying heavy baskets of ore up fragile ladders. The lucky ones died of falls rather than disease and starvation.

We stopped for the night in San Miguel de Allende near where the original plot for Mexican independence was birthed by a crazy priest and a horde of desperate and violent peasants in the early nineteenth century. We parked at the Plaza De Allende in front of La Parorquila, a strange gothic cathedral made of pink stone the color of raw meat. Supposedly, this fantasy was constructed by an Indian architect who copied the design from pictures of famous European cathedrals. Like so many other things in Mexico, it was an aberration; no beauty, just strangeness. Here, Victor Frankenstein could have conducted his experiments and sought the amalgamation of his monster. The most practical feature for the weary traveler was a cistern for holy water located on its west side. Tom claimed that it made the best urinal after dark in all Mexico.

San Miguel was what most American tourists called the good place. Old churches grew from shrubbery trimmed as close as a barbershop flattop; poncho-covered cowboys with their burros posed for tourist pictures at every corner; a fat policeman guarded the jailhouse. In the evening, gas lights pulsated around the Zocalo, strobing parading lovers like a silent movie. On the corner, an American supply store shone like a hundred plastic stars. It sold electric blenders, water purifiers, scotch, condoms, The New York Times and other necessities. San Miguel was a portable last frontier.

We spent the night in Tom's van. In the morning we threw out the empty Bohemia bottles, pissed in the cistern, and headed to the La Cucaracha Bar on the western side of the Zocalo. It had five or six wooden chairs, a couch and the decoration that gave the bar its name: a monstrous wooden cockroach. Tom was delighted.

"Now Bro, this place has character," Tom said, waving his hands across the scene. "I live here when I come to San Miguel. They say this was old Cass's hangout after it was all over, you remember him, Keoruac's buddy. They say he killed himself on the railroad tracks outside town." *On the Road* was Tom's favorite book.

"Why," I asked. I knew the story but I wanted Tom to speculate. I enjoyed making him talk. He was the only person I have ever known who could change moods in the middle of a conversation.

"Well, I figure it like this. Ole Cass just kept running until one day he outran himself. He waited for himself, got lost and died. He must have been terrified, kind of like a man who realizes that he's supposed to see his shadow on a sunny day and doesn't. Part of him was missing, the part he didn't know, and he died trying to find it."

"So he didn't find anything?"

"No, but he lost what he didn't have."

We talked about suicide, family, women, music and the sixties until the bar's action picked up. By noon, the usual patrons, a mixture of tourists, cowboys and students of the San Miguel Institute of the Creative Arts had begun to arrive. The students' conversations drifted like an autumn fog and then divided into the clarity of individual voices speaking of parts as movie extras and of novels unfinished. Like ole Cass, most of them had run too far and were trying to catch up.

We were sitting on the couch under the cockroach when a tall man who looked like a scarecrow in army fatigues pushed back the saloon doors and entered. His hair was sunset red and sprinkled with grey, and he wore a pointy-toothed, yellow smile. He resembled an elderly, insane Huck Finn. Like an angry dog prowling through a town dump, he veered across the floor toward us, then pulled up a patched chair and sat down directly facing us, his eyes hidden behind dark glasses. "Do you mind moving over a little?" he asked me. "The Corporal here needs a place to sit." He waved his left arm at thin air. I moved over.

"Waiter," the man called, snapping his fingers. No one came.

"I don't think they have waiters here," Tom said.

"Well hell, I guess service just isn't what it used to be, certainly not like in Havana. The man went to the bar and returned with a whiskey on the rocks and three beers. He placed one beer on a small table between the couch and the jukebox, by the seat that I had made vacant. Nobody laughed or turned, they just ignored the situation. I thought this must be an old joke played on new tourist, a little something to liven up the place.

"Well, speak up Corporal," Tom said. "Always nice to have a conversationalist around. I'll bet you have some interesting stories to tell."

"Where're you from?" he asked, ignoring Tom and speaking to me.

"Tuscaloosa, Alabama," I replied.

"I've been all over Alabama. I had some training at Fort Rucker. That's where I got these. He pointed at the Colonel's insignia on his left arm. "As a matter of fact, you can just call me Colonel."

"And where are you from Corporal?" Tom asked the vacant chair.

The Colonel looked at his Corporal, then after a slight pause snapped at Tom, "You deserved that. He shouldn't have told you to shut the hell up, but you can see that he's not feeling well today. His bad leg is hurting him again."

"Oh, sorry," Tom apologized sarcastically. "I'll bet that he's quite a character when he's well."

"They got him in Mexico City, but didn't finish him," the Colonel whispered, glancing over his shoulder to the south. "It was a single shot from an AK 47, that damn commie rifle. It's what they use for that sort of thing. There's too many of 'um. Can't be traced. Could be from anywhere, not like that weird old thing Oswald used.

"Who's they?" I asked. Like a nervous child peeping into a dark room, he was drawing me into his invisible game.

The Colonel shifted uncomfortably in his chair. He scanned the bar. "Castro's agents are trying to assassinate me," he reported. "I was the secret leader of the Bay of Pigs invasion. If we had won I would have been famous, and rich. That damned Kennedy didn't give us enough support." He downed his whiskey, spitting the ice back into the glass.

"So why are you in Mexico? Wouldn't you be safer back in the States?"

"I'm not exactly a hero back there. Besides, I like it here. I like the philosophy. Have you seen the mummies of Guanajuto, those twisted bodies they dug out of the peasants' cemetery?"

"No, we just got here."

"Go see them. They are in a museum behind glass for all to see. They say some natural chemical in the soil preserved them almost intact. You can feel their terror, pain and death. This country preserves those things. It Glorifies them. There's even a woman who died having a baby. Baby's still there too, hanging out of her womb." He laughed, but it was more of a gurgle from deep within his throat, hardly audible to anyone but us. "Hell, I'm more a part of this country than my own. By the way, where are you boys heading?"

"Mexico City. We have jobs there."

"Well, if you get lonely, look up a friend of mine, McNapp, he runs Happy's Pizza. He'll take care of you, the Colonel said as he got up to leave. "Goodbye boys, it's time for our siesta. Come on Corporal."

"Watch that bad leg," I said, pointing at the Corporal as they disappeared through the swinging doors.

By late afternoon we were sober and on the road to Mexico City.

As I descended from the Sierra Madres into the Valley of Mexico, I thought about Bernal Diaz del Castillo's the *True History of New Spain*, which I had been reading. This soldier of Cortez reported how, in the battle for Tenochititian and the Halls of Montecuhzoma, fifty-three Spaniards were captured, dressed with feathers and made to dance before the war god, Hultzilopochtil. Then, one by one, they had their hearts ripped out in sacrifice while their fellow soldiers watched from the causeway of Lake Texcoco. After the last screaming victim had died, their heads and those of four horses were stuck on spears and stood up facing the sun.

This had been a land of human sacrifice. The gods demanded human flesh and blood, not just any flesh, but the flesh of brave men and virgins. Unlike Civil War history prescribed by the realities of men, guns and politics, this history seemed mystical and surreal. I thought I might like it.

Following Tom, I sped into Mexico City while the Beatles sang about their Nowhere Man's lost life. But the window wind muddled the sound and blew it behind me toward the dusty, twilight sky.

4

For three weeks we lived in Tom's van parked in front of the American School. The van became our mobile home where we each carved out our own spaces. Each day we had to air it out with nature's lysol, removing the odor of human confinement.

The American School was located at Calle Sur 136, No. 135, Mexico 18 D.F., in the ground zero center of a sprawling urban slum. Its six acres were surrounded by a concrete wall with barbed-wire strung across the top, containing the students like scared soldiers in a World War I trench. An armed security guard patrolled the front gate twenty-four hours a day, and emaciated street urchins who would have made Dickens squirmish swarmed around the outside.

Most begged for pesos or sold marijuana for about two dollars a lid, some asked if they could wash the van. One small boy always tried to open Tom's door when we parked, but he was too weak. He groaned with the effort. Tom always gave him several pesos for the attempt, his tin medal. I was sickened when I saw this. I remembered the poor negroes of rural Alabama, but their lives were mostly middle class in comparison. These children lived a dirty toenail survival, living off scraps and hope.

The hillside below the school was littered with small concrete-block houses that ran together with all the symmetry of Swiss cheese. From the hilltop we could see their pink, purple, red and orange faded roofs, but if we walked toward the metro stop at the bottom, we passed around the residents' homes. There were no road maps through this zig-zag of misery. As we treaded our way down the twisting paths, the people carried on with their daily affairs. They scrubbed clothes by hand, cooked, pissed and had sex, all without regard for passers by. I thought that most of history must be like this, though it was distant from the time lines I had learned in school. We did not affect these peoples lives at all. We just flowed down the dirt and concrete hills like fingers of rainwater, dribbling through these shacks and dripping into the ditches below only to be dried by the sun and come another day, year or century.

A block from the school on Calle Constitution was Tom's favorite tienda, a small store front that sold beer, canned food, candy and poor quality meat. Every afternoon we went and drank beer in the doorway. Tom claimed he was good friends with the owner, but he couldn't pronounce his name. Tom just called him "Senor," but between us he was the "The Little Man." In his backroom The Little Man was supposed to be storing a mattress and a refrigerator Tom had bought last year from a departing friend, another teacher at the American School who had to leave quickly after he was caught smoking dope on campus during a break. Tom got them cheap.

"Shit, John," Tom moaned the afternoon we went to claim his goods. "I was supposed to bring The Little Man some real Converse tenny shoes back from the States. He really wanted them. You know

Mexico won't allow most imports. They were supposed to be his pay for taking care of my stuff. I guess I'll give him ten bucks and promise to get them at Christmas, if I go back. But it's not the same, you understand, I promised."

When we arrived at the tienda, Tom apologized profusely, but The Little Man didn't seem to care. He just waved his arms and said. "It Ok" in English, the only words he knew. The mattress was there, but the refrigerator wasn't.

After a few Bohemia Tom asked, "Donde esta me refrigerator, tu conoces?" His tone was casual so he wouldn't offend The Little Man.

He motioned for us to follow. We walked down the hill to one of the old barrio complexes and passed through a gate into a common yard surrounded by suburbs of concrete apartments, broken in places and piled into three stories like collapsed dominos. We proceeded to an apartment on the uphill side. It had a living room-bedroom unit and a small kitchen with a sink, a small wood burning stove and a refrigerator. Bed sheets were used as doors and a corner of the living area was sectioned off as a toilet area.

The Little Man led us to the refrigerator, a creaky Phillips about twenty years old. It sounded like a Cessna 50 revving its engines and misfiring. He opened it and food spilled out all over the floor. "Un momento," The Little Man said. He snapped something that I couldn't understand at one of the children who had followed us inside and slowly began to gather up the unwrapped meat and vegetables. Most of the food I couldn't identify. Within minutes, several Indian women wearing dark shawls arrived and began to pick through food like children looking for Christmas presents they knew they would not find.

"God, Tom," I murmured, handing several hunks of meat to the Indians. "This is the refrigerator for the whole neighborhood. Without it the food will spoil."

"Yeah, that's OK Senor," Tom said, motioning his hands at the women like he was trying to warn off an attack. At first, The Little

Man didn't understand. "No," Tom waved at the refrigerator. "Keep it dos semanas. Dos mas semanas." The Indian women understood that they could keep the refrigerator another two weeks, and most of them returned their food to its preserving coolness.

"Gracias," The Little Man nodded.

"We won't need it for a while," Tom said. "We can eat out. Maybe by then they will have eaten it all." They kept the refrigerator another month.

Several days later at day's early light, we were awakened by the screeching of tires and a loud thud that sounded like garbage being emptied into a city truck. "Jesus," Tom moaned as he pulled back the curtains of the van's back window. "Whatever you do, don't get out. It's dangerous to help an injured person here."

Outside, not twenty feet from the van, an old Indian woman lay dead in the street. There were chickens and penny candies scattered around her body like confetti after a parade. Her clothes were gray and black rags; but there was a single red ribbon, a pathetic reminder of a past people and their long forgotten rituals, binding her braided hair. There was no blood.

"Tom, we've got to do something," I implored, reaching for the van's door handle.

"No, we can't," Tom snatched my hand away before the lock could release. "In Mexico the authorities may hold you responsible for the person's death if you help, especially if you're a gringo and they think you have money. We should get the hell out of here. In Mexico, you ain't your brother's keeper." Tom jumped into the front seat and started the engine.

"Wait," I said, grabbing his arm. "Look."

Like shy ghosts, Indians and peasants rose out of the barrio and glided toward the still figure. One covered her with a white sheet while others placed lighted candles in a circle around the body. For a moment they prayed, and then melted into the hillside. Out of the pale light a solitary car whizzed by, weaving at the last second to avoid the incandescent shrine.

We returned three hours later for school. The woman was gone and there was no evidence she had ever lain there.

"Donde esta la mujer?" I asked one of the street children near the gate.

"La Busura," he answered.

In the garbage.

All that day Dylan rang my brain:

> *He's not selling any alibies,*
> *When you stare into the vacuum of his eyes,*
> *And he says, do you want to make a de-e-el.*
> *How does it feel to be on your own,*
> *Like a rolling stone, a complete unknown...*

5

We finally rented a house. It wasn't easy. We paid a Mexican man we knew, a property owner, to co-sign the lease. He had to swear he was our uncle. He didn't speak a word of English.

The house was in a middle class neighborhood in the city's northwest section. The street, Jimenez Y Miro, was named after a poet. I liked that. In Mexico City, if you knew your poets, generals and Aztec heroes, you could get almost anywhere. The house was a two-story stucco with a high-fenced yard, a downstairs living room with dark red caret and a fireplace, a kitchen, three bedrooms and a bathroom upstairs, and a maid's quarters on the flat roof. For us, it was luxurious.

Every week a gardener came and plied his trade for a few pesos and peasants came down from the mountains near Toluca to sell us oak wood for our fireplace. Even our garbage was a bargain.

Street children roamed from the poor sections of the city and begged for it, their shopping mall in a can.

An outside iron staircase connected the upstairs to the roof. On stormy nights in the rainy season, I often climbed up and looked north toward an unfinished bullfight arena that had steel girders sticking into the sky like giant TV antennas. Lightening sometimes struck them and shot through the open edifice like an angry Tlaocs's ammunition. Sometimes homeless street poor who had been sleeping in this modern skeleton were found dead the next morning, electrocuted, victims of the gods' anger.

To the south I could see the peaks of Popocatepetl and Ixtaccihuatl, the snow-capped volcanoes of legend. Ixtla was a lovely Aztec princess who was wooed by the warrior Popo but when he failed to win her love, he turned her to stone, and then himself as well so he might contemplate her twin-peaked breasts forever. It was a legend of failed love, something I thought I understood. Between the volcanoes is the Pass of the Eagle, where Cortez marched through on his way to destroy the ancient Mexican civilization. He did it with cannons, horses and smallpox. The frustrated lovers were lucky they missed it, petrified forever at their zenith.

On the first Sunday in our house we established a ritual: breakfast at Sanborn's off the Paseo de Reforma, a shopping trip to La Laguilla market and the bullfights. We enjoyed this because it was never the same. The unusual, the spontaneous, or the insane could emerge from one of these three events at any time. It was a ritual of the imagination and it became the testing ground for admitting newcomers to our territory.

We ate at Sanborn's, more for the ambiance than the food. Inside was a Sunday morning bacon slice of the Anglo world with American sports pages and English speaking waitresses. But framed on the wall was the famous photograph of Poncho Villa and Emilio Zapata eating here after the revolutionaries took Mexico city in December, 1914. In the picture, Villa, a violent man who loved to plunder, burn and murder, looked cheerful and drunk, his ammunition belt crossing his chest; Zapata, a principled idealist whose soldiers, hats in hand, begged for food in Mexico City's streets, looked serious and sad, his arms hanging at his sides. Both were destined for assassins' bullets.

In the center of the Paseo de Reforma outside Sanborn's front window stood a winged Nike high on a pedestal, the Monument to Independence. "Some peasants say it is a guardian angel," Tom informed me, crumbling his napkin and dropping it in his plate. "Others are waiting for an earthquake to topple it so they can steal the pieces. They think it's made of solid gold. Bullshit. Those cab racers out there would've melted it down by now."

After breakfast we went to the La Lagunilla market near the Zocalo to buy used furniture, kitchen wares and a gas stove. The Thieve's Market is its popular English name and I saw why. Streets were covered with used radios, tape players, toasters, watches, rings, purses and thousands of other items up for bargain. It looked like a thunderstorm had rained Sears and Roebuck. "You, friend," a child vendor called from behind his watch display. "The-e-e-e-s for you."

"You father ever visit Mexico?," Tom picked the watch from the child's hand and inspected its face. "It's probably his watch. You look like him. The kid probably recognizes you. His father stole it from your father."

We passed out of the department store section and by several displays of religious figures. Most were colorful two-foot wooden or plaster statutes of saints. The only one I recognized was Saint Francis and that was because he had a bird on his shoulder. All the women looked the same. "You know anything about these things?" I asked Tom.

"Hell no. Who cares. They were probably worshipped by superstitious Indian families. They're not worth anything. Why? You gonna start your own church or something?"

"No, but we could use them for some cheap artistic decoration. Besides, we haven't got anything else yet."

"Jesus, John. How many Mexican girls do you think you'll fuck under a saint's statue? You'd be better off with one of these." Tom pointed to a small booth with a plywood back wall that featured ceremonial dance masks. "These have some real spirit, Bro. And I guarantee you they'll get 'um going, bring out the primitive in 'um."

Some of the masks were simply faces of deer or rabbits, but others had hideous monster faces, obvious perversions of the ancient gods distilled with modern memory. A few, the only ones that interested me, were conquistadors with black beards and glaring eyes. "Bring on the Indian maidens, I'm ready," I called, placing one of the masks on my face and dancing a step or two.

"Watch it Bro," warned Tom. "They don't like ole Cortez much down here. They figure he raped those girls and stole their country. They think they all come from Aztec warriors."

After thirty minutes of heated bargaining, I finally bought a conquistador mask and Tom purchases a rabbit and a man's face with a lizard crawling on one cheek. The vendor charged me twice as much as Tom. I could tell he didn't want me to have Mr. Cortez. It was the only mask I ever bought, but Tom continued to buy masks every Sunday in Mexico City and at every town and village we traveled through.

The last stop was the furniture section. It was located at the permanent shops closest to the Zocalo. On Sundays, the owners set up a hodgepodge of items in the middle of the street. Unusual antiques mingled with plastic tables and chairs. One creative salesman arranged his wares by room, creating the impression of a home abandoned by its walls.

I bought a late Victorian headboard and footboard, a mattress set and a heavy frame for about fifty dollars. It was my continuing attempt to keep history alive by sleeping in it. But, Tom, for eighty dollars, bought an antique brass bed fit for a Napoleon. It was eighteenth century baroque and heavily tarnished No doubt, it was plunder from an old hacienda, a victim of revolutionary chaos. "I've always wanted one of these Bro," he beamed, rubbing his hands gently over one of its greenish rails. "I want to die in one, get struck by lightning while fucking a beautiful woman, hopefully cuming, the last shot of paradise."

We spent the last of our savings on a four-burner gas stove and a pressurized wood table with four chairs. Then we junked around and found a tapestry commemorating Lindbergh's flight and a souvenir lighter from the 1936 Hitler Olympics. We tried to bargain but the dealers guessed their worth and asked for a ridiculous price.

For lunch, we stopped at a street booth and ate several pineapple rings covered with red pepper and drank three Bohemias each. I was learning that everything in Mexico is hot, and I needed beer, lots of it, to put the fire out. But it didn't work that quickly. The first beer just spread the heat to my guts and the second one made it worse. I just kept drinking to dilute the pain. And then I ate some more.

Slightly drunk, we sped down Avenida Insurgentes to the Plaza de Mexico and the four o'clock Corrida. The Bullfights are the only event in Mexico that start on time. This has little to do with time and much to do with order. They attempt to bring order to the chaos and violence that permeate Mexican life like water pouring through gauze, and time is the apex of that order.

Tom had never seen a bullfight, but I had read "Death in the Afternoon" three times. Now it was my turn to teach. In September there aren't professional bullfights in Mexico City, only the novilladas, or amateur events. Still, the young novilladas who are going to turn professional in the winter, or in bullfight terminology, take their alternative and become full matadors, often fight better than many professionals do in season. They have more to gain.

We parked on Calle Ordin between Insurgentes and Revolucion and strolled through the pageantry of the Plaza de Mexico to the ticket windows by the main entrance. Around the Plaza, street merchants sold tacos, straw hats and bull fight paraphernalia. I was hungry but I feared the tacos, they were the color of slate. "Que es esto?" I asked an Indian woman vendor, pointing to her sizzling meat pile.

"Es pollo senor." She wiped grease-drenched hands on her dirty apron.

"More like burro than chicken," I observed, sniffing at the smoky air.

"It's good for ya Bro. Just think of all that protein." Tom cocked his right arm, exposing his bicep. "Why I'll bet these mothers tell their children, 'eat your donkey and you'll grow up big and strong. Just think of all the starving children in Africa with no donkey to eat.'"

I stepped into the ticket mob and asked for two in the Sombra section close to the action.

"Hey you there, would ya get us tickets too. We don't speak Spanish." A girl with black hair and an Italian nose pushed her way beside me. She was wearing a blue-jean skirt and a tight red sweater. Her breast bulged like soccer balls beneath the open neckline. "I'm Sharon and that's Vanessa." She pointed to an attractive skinny girl with big oval eyes standing by the gate. She looked like an attractive Olive Oil waiting to be saved by Popeye.

"Why not," I said, nodding towards Tom. "He's with me."

There were no close tickets in the shade, so I bought seats in the Sol section on the third row. Neither of the girls was Lady Bret but they were available. Sharon chose me and Vanessa picked Tom, random pairing and I don't think any of us understood the criterion. It was just the way things floated into place in this evaporating steam of sexual relations. We bought a round of Corona draft beers and took our seats. Across in the Sombra section were several bus loads of tourists with floppy hats and cameras.

Inside, the Plaza de Mexico is a gigantic funnel: noise, light, action, sight and feeling pour from the wide circle of the high seats into the narrow confines of the arena. "Why it's a perfect circle." Sharon's eyes scanned it. "There's nowhere for the poor bull to get away."

"He's not supposed to get away. He's supposed to die," I corrected.

"But that's not fair. He should have an equal chance."

"No he shouldn't. Think of the bullfight as a three-act play with the ending always the same. The first two acts prepare the bull for the final act, the faena, which results in the ritualistic death of the bull. The bull is a sacrifice to art. The plot is the same but the matador is the writer who must create the dialogue. He writes with his cape." I felt very erudite explaining this anachronism. I was trying to read more into it than men, blood and cheap entertainment.

"But can't he do all that without killing the bull?"

"No. The aesthetic unity of the drama demands that the bull be killed." I wasn't sure why but Mr. Hemingway had said so. I hoped she wouldn't pursue the subject. I didn't want an argument. I wanted this entertainment to lead between her legs.

Tom and Vanessa weren't arguing. He pointed to attractions in the stands while Vanessa gurgled and laughed in her beer. I was pissed. I felt the bullfights were a serious business. After all, here we had men facing death away from life's comic pursuits. This was bare minimum life, this death business, and I wanted everyone to know it. I knew that I liked bullfighting more than football, and I think my father would've too.

At exactly four o'clock the music sounded and the novilleros and their assistants, the cuadrilla, paraded to the center of the ring. The ceremonial official, the alguacilillo, received the President's orders, and then the cuadrilla dispersed in orderly lines to the safety of the fence, or barrera. Then the first bull charged into the empty arena. He was a squatty black creature with humpy muscles like rolling hills. While several members of the cuadrilla, the peons, spread their capes to study his movement, the bull ran helter-skelter, often falling when a front leg gave way, driving his face into the sand.

"He's not a good bull," I said to Tom. "He's too jerky and he has poor balance."

"Kind of runs like me, with his left side a little twisted," he replied.

After watching for several minutes, Hector Rodriguez, a tall blond Spaniard in his early twenties and the first novillero, led the bull to the center of the ring and with his large pink cape performed three decent veronica passes to a rising chorus of "oles." Becoming almost flat and parallel to the ground, the cape spun around his body like a magic carpet as the confused bull confronted only air. "That pass is named after Saint Veronica who offered a cloth to wipe the perspiration from the savior's face," I explained. "In a symbolic way the matador offers this pass to the crowd." I felt religious, as if I were peering into something beyond me and my past.

"Oh God, is he handsome," cried Sharon. "Look at that outfit, who's his tailor anyway." She was referring to the novillero's sparkling suit of lights, or traje de luces. Hector Rodriguez's was trimmed in gold. I wasn't impressed. I thought it made him look like a gaudy rock star playing for pieces from the girls.

"Somebody must have poured him into that thing," Vanessa observed.

He ended his first act with a beautiful serentina pass, the cape twirling smoothly over the top of his head like a coiling snake. The crowd shouted "oles".

"I thought you said he was a bad bull, Bro," Tom said.

"He was. But this novillero is turning him into a good one. He's studying the defects and using them to his advantage. He knows he has a bull that loves to charge and he's making the best of it."

"I can relate to that" Vanessa said, passing Tom an invitation with her eyes.

"I know how to handle men who love to charge" Sharon said.

"But do you kill them," I asked.

"Only for fun, not for art."

As the corrida fight continued, I explained to my own little cuadrilla how the picadores weakened the bull with a pic thrust and how the banderilleros enlivened the bull again by planting their colorful little sticks into the bulls back. One banderillero was thrown by the bull and limped off slightly bruised. There were no complaints from Tom or the girls, in fact, they were clapping, shouting "oles" and becoming part of the event. Then Hector Rodriguez entered the arena for the faena. He took his small cape, the muleta, from an assistant, bowed to the President, and threw his hat to a senora seated in the front row of the sombra seats.

He approached the bull from the front, holding the cape in his left hand. Like a busty girl in a beauty pageant, he stuck out his chest and strutted toward the bull, shouting, "Toro, Toro." The bull charged tentatively and Rodriguez passed the bull in quarter turns close to his body. Rhythmically, he glided the animal into half-circles and then finally into a full circle, the bull wrapping around his body like a blanket. Rodriguez's feet and body were motionless as he controlled the bull with only his extended arm, a classic natural pass. The "oles" were one tenor voice as he ended by passing the bull close by his chest, the dangerous pase de pecho.

"Jesus, that was like moving sculpture," Tom said, mesmerized. I knew he was thinking of himself and how to make his own sculpture. Sharon and Vanessa were on their feet clapping and bouncing.

Rodriguez acknowledged the "oles" with a flip of his head and a smile while he pranced to the barrera to receive his sword for the kill, the estocada. "Now, this is the most important of the drama," I continued my instruction, snapping my fingers for another Corona to be delivered. "He must kill the bull on the first attempt. That way the bull's death means something. It fought a courageous battle and the crowd expects the matador to deliver him a noble death. The sword must pass between his horns and the matador must clear the bull by passing to his side at the last possible second. And the bull must die quickly."

"I don't want to see it," Vanessa whined as Rodriguez aimed his sword, but Sharon watched intently.

Hector Rodriguez failed. The bull lifted his head and the sword hit muscle instead of the soft spot that led to the heart. It flew in the air and bounced over the barrera. The bull bucked in a frenzy, the spell broken. The stage curtain had stayed up too long. Rodriguez tried again with similar results. There were a few disapproving whistles and some tourists in the Sol seats began to leave. Finally, on the third attempt, he plunged in to the hilt. The bull staggered toward the barrera, blood pouring from his mouth. I heard the Mexicans behind me comment that Rodriguez got him in the lung.

The bull refused to die and after several long minutes, Rodriguez finished it by severing the spine with a dagger. Many people in the crowd stood and clapped, acknowledging the muleta work. Several white handkerchiefs waved from the tourist section requesting that he be awarded an ear. The President granted this request and Rodriguez received his ear from the alguacilillo and began his walk around the ring. Flowers landed at his feet. He picked them up off the bloody dirt, kissed them and threw them back into the crowd. As he neared us a bra and some keys were offered but he ignored them.

"Damn it, what can I throw," Sharon yelled. "I want him to notice me." She sat down and deftly slipped off her panty and threw it at Rodriguez. It hit him in the head and landed on his shoulder. He laughed and put it in his jacket.

"Why don't you throw him a ruler too," Tom joked. "He might be the only spic here who could use one."

The remaining fights were havoc without the excellent cape and muleta work that distinguished the first one. There were no ears cut, only bloody kills and a sense of waste. The other two novilleros were boys who ran whenever the bull got close. One tried to excite the crowd by fighting barefooted and on his knees, but he spent most of his time diving and running. Still, Sharon's exuberance about Hector Rodriguez's first fight was not affected. "I didn't know death could be so much fun," she said as we left the Plaza.

6

We took the girls to eat at a clean looking tacoria restaurant off Calle Rodin. It was nearly filled with local bullfight aficionados; we were the only foreigners. As we walked inside I heard "Gringo" muttered from an unidentified table. However, the owner came from behind the counter, introduced himself and ushered us to a table. I could tell he was pleased to serve us. I spoke in Spanish and translated for the girls. He suggested we have his specialty: grilled goat tacos. Vanessa glanced at the goat turning slowly on the rotisserie and said softly, "I don't think so."

Instead, we had three rounds of Bohemias and stuffed ourselves on Tacas al Carbon, the Central Mexican specialty made of pork cooked on an upright rotisserie and flavored with pineapple and sharp yellow cheese. There were three flavors of hot sauce ranging from mild guacamole to the superhot red-peppered picante. I asked the owner, Senor Bueno, for his hottest, the sauce "caliente." "No senor," he corrected. "You want sauce picante especial. Caliente applies only to fires and women, you understand." He winked and rolled his eyes toward Sharon.

"Si, I understand," I answered.

"Hey, take us somewhere and show us some history, Mr. Teacher," Sharon ordered as she downed her last Bohemia. "And I have something that's as hot as these tacos, that is, if you boys smoke. I brought it straight from New York on the plane. They didn't even check me."

"They check you going out, not coming in," Tom signaled for the tab. "And leaving they get you both ways so you better be careful. The U.S. Feds are yelling about drugs in Mexico coming across the border and the Mexicans are nailing a few tourists to make it look like they're doing something."

Senor Bueno refused to accept our money. He was playing "El Patron," meaning he was being generous to his new friends and showing he was a man of status. Many small restaurant owners went broke this way; there weren't always paybacks.

We left a tip that was more than the bill and stumbled out into the late afternoon drizzle. Erie red halos hung around the streetlights due to mist and pollution. We had gone only a block when Senor Bueno came running up behind us carrying Tom's Pentax camera. "El Patron" was an honest man.

Tom weaved the van. It moved like a fat angry snake through the chaotic Insurgentes traffic which seemed to take on a life of its own, each driver becoming the predator of another's frustrations. We turned into the Paseo de Reforma, spun around Glorieta Chauhtemoc circle and the Monument de Independencia, and arrived at Chapultepec Park. Like soldiers fleeing a surprise attack, the driving was frantic. There were no marked lanes, so I called "red" or "green" to identify the proper lane and escape the Glorieta circles. I visualized a purgatory where a cowardly driver goes around forever, wide-eyed and terrified. We saw a 1955 Ford die on the street, coughing in a pillow of smoke. The driver got out, kicked the car once, and walked away. Stripped to its chassis, it was still there a week later, a monument to the apocalypse.

Tom parked the van and we climbed half-way up the hill behind Chapultepec Castle. Here were large boulders surrounded by foliage that provided hiding places for the Sunday Mexican lovers who came to make love away from their crowded homes. The castle had served as the resident of the Emperor Maximillan and his queen Charlotte. They had longed for a kingdom so Napoleon III of France put them on the throne by force to serve as his puppet monarchs. Maximillan was shot by Juarez as an example to the world not to meddle in Mexican affairs. Charlotte returned to Europe and died insane at the age of ninety.

We sat on an old patchwork quilt between two boulders and took turns shooting Tequila Sauza with lime and salt. It was good against the night chill. Sharon lit up a joint, inhaled deeply and passed it around. "Not bad for commercial stuff," Tom said, after a few hits. "You tried any mota here."

Both girls shook their heads. "Got any," Sharon asked.

"Yeah we got some back at the house. It's easy and cheap down here. We buy it from the street kids, flower tops and all. It comes from around the volcanic fields near Popo. It's only about two dollars a lid and it'll knock your top off."

"Even mine," Sharon asked in mock surprise.

"Yeah, even yours."

We smoked another joint and finished the tequila. Tom and Vanessa kissed and began rubbing one another's legs. Sharon and I found a secluded spot nearby and she gave me a speedy blow job, obviously enjoying it more than me, but I was too numb from the dope and tequila to cum. I knew it would take more. All I could think about was old Maximillan and his last words when they shot him, "Viva Mexico!" I'm glad he couldn't see that in the future four stoned, drunk and horny gringos would use the back of his house for a late afternoon's entertainment. He gave his life for his dreams, but we were eluding ours. Sharon had found her history, but we sure as hell weren't giving it any respect.

It was dark and beginning to rain by the time we arrived at the house. We lit candles around the living room and pulled the curtains even though there was no one who could see us. Sharon and Vanessa rolled one of our Mexican joints while Tom opened the red Santo Tomas wine and I built a fire to cure the cool dampness. We drank this cheap wine from the bottle and passed around the joint while the fire crackled. I felt the scorching fingers of pot reach into my lungs. Conversation became meaningless and I faded into the fire.

The Aztecs were there, dancing around the Great Pyramid in celebration. Children were playing games of hide-and-seek in the watching crowd and the pastels of Tenochtitlan were glowing softly in the fading light of the setting sun beyond the mountains. A full moon was rising in the east on the pyramid's apex. I was stretched on the sacrificial alter awaiting the plunge of the black-robed priest's obsidian knife that would tear out my heart as a sacrifice to the gods. I was struggling, not going willingly, as a good warrior should who knew that his death would help bring back the sun, rain and wind. Beside me was a princess, clothed in white robes stained with blood below her waist. She was awaiting the sacrifice with calm, open eyes.

I was jolted awake when Sharon jumped up and removed her sweater. "I want to dance," she shouted, turning pirouettes. "And I want to dance naked. Put on something I can dance to."

I struggled to the tape player and put on the Eagles. She stripped and began dancing naked among us like a Go-Go dancer at a happy hour, sometimes stopping to rub my face with her breast or hunch slowly in my face to the hard electric:

> *Movin, can't you see she wants you,*
> *She has you deep in her eyes.*
> *You been, wondering why she haunts you,*
> *Beauty in the devil's disguise.*

This was no Evelyn with love sentiments and sex woven into an intricate web by a patient, poisonous spider. Sharon grasped the wine bottle by the neck and slowly dripped wine over her body, massaging it into her silver-dollar nipples:

> *Higher, she can keep you loaded feeding you*
> *whisky and wine.*
> *Fire, the devil's on the phone,*
> *He laughs and said you're doing just fine...*

Behind her I saw birds in the fire. Their black wings stretched outward as they soared out and over her, swirling in a solid ring around my head. Carlota screeched upstairs, a voice from the desert. Sharon danced behind me and rested her breast on my shoulders while her hands rubbed my chest from behind. I felt her long nails, sharp as ice-picks, stab over my heart. For a second the cold fear that I was about to become an Aztec sacrifice chilled me:

> *In that big book of names*
> *I'm gonna go down in flames,*
> *seein's how I'm going down...*

Tom led Vanessa upstairs. Sharon and I stayed. She took me with slow hunches that rose slowly like the noise of a distant approaching train. I felt myself rise out of my body and watch us, as divorced from the action as someone walking in during the middle of a television re-run. Then I slipped back into myself and came. Blood trickled down my chest and Sharon slowly licked it off:

> *Oh well, it's been a good day in hell,*
> *Tomorrow I'll be glory bound.*

7

Our fellow employees at the American School treated Tom and me like we were some new and interesting virus which was interesting to study and discuss but too dangerous to be around. Most of the teachers were burned out romantic ex-patriots who in a spasm of insanity married Mexicans, had kids, and became twilight Americans. Their idea of freedom was a Nieman-Marcus shopping trip to Houston or a Dallas Cowboys football game on their expensive cable televisions. They envied our John Wayne gaits and loose energy and they resented us because we refused to participate in their country club parties, adulterous affairs, or hypocritical reminiscences filled with the jargon of the dispossessed about the good lives they left behind in New York, Detroit or Los Angeles.

The school's director was Felicia Goldstein, a plump, dyed red-headed Jewish woman from New York in her late forties who resembled a frog. Despite being semi-literate in Spanish and English, she claimed she was writing a history of Mexico's 1910 revolution. She once stomped into my history class and berated me for correcting the poor grammar in my students' history papers. "What's this," she yelled, waving one of my graded papers like a saber. "You're stifling their creativity. You should only be interested in the facts."

"They can't interpret the facts unless they can write," I protested. "They must be able to explain their ideas."

"Write! Write! You are saying that James Joyce couldn't write." She threw the paper on my desk. "He didn't know grammar and look at him."

"He knew it perfectly. That's why he could break the rules to create his own style," I said, arguing with the power of my English minor.

"We'll see about this," she threatened, her fat tongue searching for flies as she hopped away.

And she liked Tom even less. One day early in the school year she called us both to her office. "Tom," she began as she squinted at him from behind her glasses. "It has been reported that you and your roommate here are having wild drug parties and orgies at your little hacienda and that some students are involved. What do you have to say about this?"

"No way, Miss Goldstein," Tom replied, feigning surprise. "The only grass in our house is the woven chairs we bought on Avenida Insurgentes. Besides, John here is from an honorable old Southern family and he doesn't allow that sort of thing in his presence." Tom knew Miss Goldstein, a University of Michigan graduate, hated Southerners.

"And what's this I hear about the students?" she continued, pushing her glasses down the bridge of her nose and peering at Tom over their frame. "It has been reported that you have been holding hands with Linda Blakney on the school campus."

"Aw, Miss Goldstein," Tom whined shyly. "You know if I was guilty I'd be doing more than holding hands."

"I want you two to know something," she croaked. "There are some student teachers coming in soon from Minnesota. I want you to stay away from them. I don't want them to get the wrong impression of this school and its community. Do you understand?"

"Yes Ma'am," Tom drawled sarcastically. We certainly wouldn't want them to think poorly of our little school here now would we?"

Outside the office door Tom did a quick jig. "Hot damn, student teachers," he chuckled, throwing his long hair behind his ears. "We'll get to them the first day they're here. There's bound to be two lookers in the crowd. Maybe they can live with us and split the rent."

"Tom, you heard the Frog. If we get close to them we'll be fired."

"No way Bro. No teacher's gonna drag ass to Mexico in the middle of the semester. There's nobody to take our place. We're safe for this year, and we'll worry about next year, next year. And besides that, the Frog likes me. I tell her she looks pretty every day. Believe me, she's just jealous."

There were a few kindred souls who liked us and made life at the school tolerable. The most unique was Tilly LaTell, a former Irish nun who had worked as a nurse with the Mayas. She had come out of her order and was teaching psychology, dating a young matador and writing poetry. She was in her early forties, had a marvelous figure, deep green eyes and dark red hair. Her small downtown apartment didn't have a kitchen and Tilly spent long hours cooking elaborate meals for us at our house on holidays. She said she did it for relaxation. Also, she was our nurse. When the bumps, bangs and fevers of our tumultuous lives in Mexico got the best of us, it was Tilly who soothed the pain. I suppose we were easier than the Mayas. I was attracted to her and so, I think, was Tom. But, I also think there was some invisible wall that prevented either of us from attempting a sexual relationship with her. It wasn't fear of rejection: it was a fear of consummation.

Our other school chum was the eccentric football coach, Captain John Coles. His wishbone high school football teams dominated the Mexico City league and a few schools from Texas. He named his half-Mexican son Bryant after his idol, coach Bear Bryant of Alabama, and he spent every afternoon he could watching again and again the film of his team's greatest victory over their archrival, Tepayac. He was about 6'3", 260 pounds, bald as a desert mountain and he didn't attempt the pure-life image that many coaches falsify. Not a day went by that he didn't whisper to one of us, "Pisst, you see the tits on Lisa today. She's not wearing a bra. I'm supposed to send her home, but I'm going to wait until after lunch." At least once a week he loved to escape his crowded Mexican household where several families lived and come to our house for a cold beer and conversation. Coach Coles wasn't in the best of circumstances, but he lived his life like a fat, happy beaver gnawing at a tree. That's why we liked him.

Despite the Frog and her dim associates, I loved teaching at the American School. I taught World History using the inquiry method. The students examined historical events by asking WHO, WHAT, WHERE, WHEN, HOW, AND WHY. Through this socratic questioning and analysis, they were supposed to seek the meaning of events and not just memorize the facts. They were supposed to interpret the world for themselves, something that was giving me trouble. However, it was easy. I could hide in history during the school day and at three o'clock leave the interpretation in closed books. I had more personal things to work on.

The students were active and bright, Some, like Illana Perez, who had served in the six-day Arab-Israeli war as a nurses aide, had survived gutsy experiences in the real world. In the loose, Latin atmosphere, I soon became friends with many of them and we often went to lunch at the Little Man's store to drink wine and discuss the lesson.

Tom became even better friends with certain students. Several of the most attractive senior girls saw him to be an excellent confessor for their boyfriend problems, and the most serious confessions took place in Tom's bedroom. All day he fought seventh and eighth grade brats with clay and crayons. In the afternoons he left school warning, "I almost killed a kid today. Tomorrow, I'm gonna throw little Danny Shithead in the kiln and bake him along with the ashtrays." After these battles, Tom felt the senior girls were his combat pay.

Tom's favorite was the infamous Linda Blakney about whom even the frog had heard. Linda was a freckled-faced and red-headed teen with alluring green eyes that gave her an evil beauty beyond her years. Tom romanced her with flowers and flattery and preyed upon his image as an attractive older artist in search of a younger inspiration. However, unlike her peers, Linda treated Tom like a toy. She accepted his admiration but withheld her ample charms. Tom went crazy. He began to listen to songs alone with his goggle-eyed imagination as the only companion. He praised her intelligence and creativity repeatedly, once even showing me a story that she had written that he declared was the "best damned short story he had ever read."

It was indeed excellent. In fact, it was so good that I recognized it. "Tom, this story was lifted from Truman Capote's novel *OTHER VOICES, OTHER ROOMS*. It's about a kid's tortured, growing personality. I studied it in my Southern Literature course."

"That's bullshit, John. You have just never liked her."

I went upstairs and returned with the book, one of the many I had brought to Mexico, and showed him the chapter. It was the carnival scene. He read it silently for a few minutes. "And why, John, do you suppose she did this? She told me it was hers. She even submitted this story to her English teacher."

"To be more than she is, or what she is. You better be careful Tom."

I always left whenever Linda came over. Tom thought she would feel more comfortable with him alone. One day in late September he asked me to leave. "Today's the day Bro. I've been waiting a long time for this."

And it was the day, but it didn't turn out the way Tom had it figured. When I returned to the house late on a Saturday afternoon, I saw Linda step outside the gate and shove a lavish bouquet into Tom's face and storm off laughing. Tom just stood there, still as the Nike Monument on Reforma while flower petals floated onto his shoulders like dandruff.

"She just laid there like a piece of plywood Bro," he moaned over a few Bohemias that night at supper. "She kept her eyes open and looked straight at me with a smile on her face, then, when I finished, she said 'is that all' and laughed. She screwed me man, and it was my own fault. I can't believe I acted that way about her."

Tom's lesson wasn't lost on me. Whenever I was attracted to a student at the school, I remembered Linda Blakney.

8

Several days a week after school, we drove downtown to the Zona Orsa to explore the city and drink Bohemias at the El Vaso de Oro, our favorite sidewalk cafe. Here we sat and watched the surreal people of this strange survival town wander by our table. We felt empathy for the lost-looking travelers carrying backpacks and needing showers. Sometimes, we bought these folks a beer and advised them about the best food and the most places to visit. We attempted to give them an hour's initiation into Mexico City's random world. Some didn't listen. They just wanted to slide. Mexico was the end of a long toilet flush where they could spin down the final sewer of despair.

One day in early October, we spied the Colonel sitting alone at a table by the street corner. "Come on," Tom said. "Let's move over there and see what the crazy ole bastard is up to."

"May we join you," I asked as we approached his table. "That is, if the Corporal here doesn't mind." I pointed to the empty chair.

"What's wrong with you," he retorted sharply. "The Corporal's not here. He's dead. They got him in a crowd at the Zocolo here during the September 5th Independent Day celebrations. A sniper shot him in the head." In his left hand, the Colonel was fingering cloth stripes with frayed edges, obviously ripped off a uniform. "These were his. It was all they would let him wear. No medals for his missions. But go ahead and have a seat. What's over is over." The Colonel wasn't wearing fatigues, Instead, he wore jeans with a black tee-shirt, cowboy boots, and, despite the overcast sky, his dark glasses. His only military marking was a baseball cap that read MARINES.

"Sorry to hear about the Colonel," Tom sympathized. "Who do you think shot him, the Commies?"

"It could have been anybody, the Commies, business rivals, anybody, even our own people." The Colonel picked up a menu and scanned the selections. "But why be sorry? He died in the line of duty. Duty is something to die for. It's when you die for nothing that's sad, or somebody else makes you die for nothing. That's the way it is here in Mexico. People celebrate death for death's sake. It's in their souls. It's part of their lives. Stick around long enough and you'll see."

"I don't plan on sticking around here long enough to see," Tom said.

"You'll see," the Colonel repeated. "Incidentally, did you ever get over to Happy's Pizza to see my friend McNapp?"

"No, we forgot. We'll get over there soon," I answered.

"You know, he's a pretty successful businessman. And he likes Americans. You could probably pick up some extra money working for him in some way. He always needs some kind of help, in a business way I mean. You teachers don't make much, do you?"

"We do OK," I answered. "We'll stop by for pizza, but we don't want any jobs just yet. We need the time."

"Oh, well, whatever," he said, shrugging. "But if you do see him don't forget to give him my regards and tell him I'll be by soon. Excuse me, fellows, but I've got an appointment to keep." The Colonel paid in advance for a round of Bohemias and left, glancing around the corner before he turned and walked toward Insurgentes. He was an eccentric, sure, but I felt here was a man who had some stories to tell. For a while, he had me almost believing in the Corporal. I imagined a dead bird dangling from his neck as he walked away.

It was because of the El Vaso de Oro that our house became a refuge for burned-out gypsies. Every afternoon beginning in October, I went to the Zona Rosa for intensive Spanish lessons at the Escuela de Cultura. Some days Tom came along to hold court at the Vaso de Oro with these last remains of the sixties, people who like Bob Dylan's answers were *Blowin' in the Wind.* However, these people were more like dead pollen caught in dust devils. They floated about in dry swirls of confusion, fertilizing nothing.

First there was Shotgun, whose boyfriend was serving seven years in Lecumberri Penitentiary for smuggling marijuana. She swore she was going to live in Mexico City until his release. "I'm here to deliver his money, groceries, mail and pussy," she proclaimed. "He has to have me to live. I'm his salvation. I have some money my aunt left me. With it he can keep a private cell furnished like a hotel room. He even has plants. And for a fifty-dollar bribe, I can have a fuck visit once a week."

Shotgun didn't look worth fifty-dollars a year. She was short, pale and skinny with long stringy brown hair that hung like wet ropes to her waist. Her eyes were a faded blue surrounded by a jaundiced yellow, probably the result of what was left of the needle tracks on her arms. For days at a time she wore the same ankle-length gingham dress and a blouse embroidered with colorful plumed birds. Her sandles were Mexican guaraches with Goodyear soles. She wasn't too old, certainly not past her late twenties, but she looked as ageless as the Indian woman selling trinkets in the streets. Strangely, she gave the impression of having once been pretty, way back before the eve of destruction.

"I need a place to stay," she pleaded, nervously rummaging through her sack purse and pulling out a handful of unexchanged twenties. "I can't afford to pay you now because all of this is for him. But I can buy groceries and dope. Just don't try and fuck me. That's not my scene anymore."

Tom took me aside for a decision. "What the hell. I'll bet that she'll leave soon anyway," he reasoned. I was surprised. Tom was usually the one in control. I had been following his paths blindly, letting him shop his way through the choices.

"Jesus, Tom. We aren't running a dog pound. Her type looks like trouble."

"Well, look at it this way. She's kind of on a pilgrimage for love. We can help her a little. What do ya say?" Tom put his hand on my shoulder and leaned slightly towards me.

"OK," I relented. "And who cares if she fucks us. Look at'er. She pitiful."

Shotgun moved in that night.

Our next house guest was Squid, a malarious rail who had just returned from Africa with a ton of beads, carvings, pottery and trinkets. Squid had his merchandise shipped to Guadalajara, Oaxaca and Mexico City. He planned to arrive in each city, claim his goods at customs and trade them at the local markets for silver and turquoise jewelry. Next, he planned to sell these products to businesses in California. Somewhere in all of this was a profit, but Squid didn't plan very well. He didn't plan on Mexican customs. They wanted five thousand dollars duty for his twenty boxes in Mexico City, just his first stop.

"Man, I can rig it," Squid predicted. "I've rapped with this customs agent, Raul something-another. He promised me that for about a thousand bills he can get my stuff released." Squid dug into his burritos, the specialty of El Vaso de Oro. He talked while he chewed, the salsa dripping from his mouth into his lap and spotting him like a case of measles. "It'll just take about a week or so to complete things. Say, can I stay with you guys? I'll give you some of my African stuff when I get it. Heck, take you pick. Some of that stuff is really valuable, even has some magic powers, medicine man stuff you know, cures anything. How about it, huh?"

"Sure, I really dig African sculpture. That's what got Picasso started." Tom turned to me. "How about you Bro?"

I was more comfortable with Squid than with Shotgun. He obviously didn't have both oars in the water but he was one of us, a wayfarer trying to make things work with a morbid lost innocence. "No problem Squid. Welcome to Mexico."

The last member of our El Vaso de Oro family was Margarita, my first Mexican lover. Every night after work she sashayed past our table with a body like a Penthouse centerfold and a head full of curly black hair that reminded me of an untrimmed poodle. The Mexican men paid her little attention because they preferred women with hips large enough to drive a truck between and BB-sized breasts, just the opposite of Margarita. But we sure as hell noticed. "Oye, senorita, como estas," Tom called every time she swung by.

"Muy bein, e tu," she responded one day, stopping by an empty chair. I quickly got up and pulled the chair out, motioning for her to sit down. She lit a cigarette with a fake mother-of-pearl lighter and began sucking on the plastic holder with rounded lips until the smoke slithered upward in a solid line. "Me llama Margarita, y tu?" she asked casually.

"Bro, it's going to be a long afternoon," Tom said. "I don't believe she speaks a word of English."

"Si ah speeeka EEnnglish." She moved her eyes about and struck a distracted pose, turning her nose slightly up in the air and giving her hair a slip off the neck. "Seee, as sing. 'And when I touch you I feel happy inside, it's such a feeling of my love I can't hid mmmmmm.'" Her foot twitched under the table, bumping mine.

"I see what you mean," I said. Many Mexican girls who couldn't speak or understand English had memorized dozens of the songs they heard. In fact, Margarita didn't speak a word of English. We communicated with a combination of poor Spanish and gestures. But I was enthralled. She had the rough beauty of a thunderstorm and I knew I wanted her. I had dreamed of making love to an Indian princess and here she was, ready for the conquest. Del Castillo had written how Cortez always had the pick of the local women. Until now, I had felt more like a private taking the leftovers. Here was my opportunity.

Margarita had a job as a manicurist at a Zona Rosa salon. Lacking education and with many impossible dreams, she had moved from the rural south to Mexico City, where she hoped to become a starlet. She told us she had appeared in fashion magazines and belonged to an exclusive tennis club in Polanco, but any fool could see her self-portrait, painted with wild colors but without background.

My Indian princess attacked me that very night. I never had a chance. She became a lighting bolt striking everything and most dangerous near the thunder. She grabbed personal possessions and waved them about shouting, "Que es este" She bounced on our beds until the springs popped and she dug through our favorite tapes and played one verse of every song on every other tape spewing words in guttural Spanish like ancient Ixtla spewed lava. "Calma te, Calma te," Tom pleaded. She really got on his nerves. And she physically abused us, charging from one to the other biting our ears, necks or lips with all the sensuousness of an angry tigress. "God", screamed

Tom. "She bit through my ear." He stared at his bloody fingers. "She's crazy, the bitch."

"You warned me about these women," I laughed. "Now it's time for me to find out myself. This one's mine."

"Fine, just keep her away from me."

"Yes sir, Capitan," I saluted.

I finally guided my princess to my bedroom and shut the door. She pranced to my conquistador mask on the wall and asked, "Quein es este?" From behind, I circled her waist with my arms. "Es mi." Suddenly she turned, grabbed the back of my head and pressed her lips to mine so hard I tasted blood, mine. Then, like a clear-up hitter gripping a Louisville slugger, she shoved her hands down my pants and grabbed me. "Oh shit," I yelled.

"Yo te quiero," she gurgled, saliva muffling the sound.

"Si, I want you too," I huffed while I removed her tight white slacks.

We fell into bed without pants but still with tops. I reached for her blouse but her strong hands stopped me. "No Johnny," she said and rolled me over, straddling me like a professional wrestler. I was driven inside her as she bit my ears, shoulders and neck so hard I felt her teeth meet. Her muscles grasped and pulled me even deeper. "Ahhh, punta me, punta me," she cried.

Afterwards I collapsed, sore and exhausted. Margarita leapt up and banged on the wall. "Tomas, Tomas," she called. There was no answer. Still pantless, she charged into Tom's bedroom. I heard her spring on his bed. "No," he screamed. "Get the fuck out of here."

"Don't worry Tom," I consoled through the wall. "The Aztecs only sacrificed virgins. You'll be alright."

Margarita became mine, or I became hers. But she only stayed two nights a week. That was all anybody could take, even Squid.

Tilly was concerned about my quick relationship with Margarita. She had met her at dinner the weekend after the conquest. They had spoken cooley, shortly, and Margarita had kept her distance from Tilly.

"She's just not for you, John," Tilly said, pouring more coffee into my cup. "She's a peasant. You don't have anything in common."

"I don't need anything in common. I've had that before." She knew all about Evelyn. I got up and shut the door to the teacher's lounge. I didn't want anyone snooping in our private lives. "And what about Ramon, your matador. Are you taking up bullfighting?"

"That's different. He's an educated Spaniard and we speak each other's languages fluently. He also writes poetry. You and Margarita can't even understand each other. You are toys for each other to play with and sex is the only one you share. And every relationship carries some kind of responsibility, whether you want it or not." Her voice was as soft as cotton. I never knew Tilly to argue.

"Is this Tilly the nun speaking?"

"No, Tilly the friend. Slow down, make things count. Evelyn made the mistake, you didn't. There's nothing to make-up for. She served herself a less generous helping. I'm just concerned about you, that's all. Margarita may even be a prostitute. Salons on the edge of Zona Rosa employ country peasants to make extra money, sex goes with the massage."

"She's a manicurist."

"No, I think she's a masseuse. Look at the muscles in her hands."

"Well, I'm not too concerned she doesn't speak the mother tongue. I understand enough. And I like her strong hands."

The bell rang and we returned to our morning classes. I trusted Tilly but I just didn't care what or who Margarita was. I was the one who counted and she could be a chapter in my personal history book, or at least an illustration.

9

Mexico City began celebrating November 1, The Day of the Dead, weeks early. All through October the crafts shops in the Zona Rosa and San Angel market displayed smiling papier-mache skeletons and ghoulish renditions of people in various stages of dying. Neighborhood bakeries sold sweet sugar versions of monsters for the children to lick and in the cemeteries, even the stoneless pauper's graves began to attract flowers and food. A festival had begun.

At our house there were creeping problems. Shotgun was having trouble visiting Michael in Lecumberri prison. "I couldn't believe it," she told us during a Sunday night fireside chat. "The matron took my bribe and then allowed the guards to search me. Two of them felt me up. One greasy bastard with rotten teeth shoved his finger up my twat. And then they made me pay an extra fifty-dollars to spend the night with Michael. So I had to give him my last expense money as a bribe so Michael could keep his private cell. That's got to last him the rest of the month. I'm afraid of what could happen to him."

"I thought you had plenty of money," I reminded her. "Enough to last seven years."

"I lied," she replied. "Maybe enough to last until Christmas."

Despite the cold night air, there were beads of sweat on her forehead. Her milky eyes, mesmerized by concern, stared straight into the fire. Until now I had suspected her dedication was a lie, just a ragged diversion to escape going back to the States. But now I saw that she had a true dedication, although it was to herself. After what must have been a soiled life, this was a last attempt to find a goodness inside that until now had been hidden in a high or a rush.

"What the fuck," Squid interrupted. "I'll loan you a few bucks when I get my shit." He slid closer to the fire. "Jesus, I haven't been this chilled since I got the fever in Africa."

"I'd loan you some money, Shotgun," I offered truthfully. "But I just don't have it. Of course you're free to stay here as long as you want and you don't have to pay for food. It doesn't cost any more to feed one more mouth here in Mexico."

"Thank you, you're both so good," she said softly. "But it wouldn't matter. I need something over the long haul. I've got to help him survive for seven years. I've applied for jobs at the embassy, some schools and cultural centers. I dropped out of college, but I think I can fake a degree if a teaching job comes my way. I can't type, but maybe I could answer the phone somewhere. I could learn Spanish in no time I'm sure. I could scrimp and save and help him through this time."

"And then," I asked.

"And then," she repeated sadly.

And the sad sounds of another salvation rang from the stereo:

... and she buy-y-y-y-ing a stairway to heaven.

The last weeks of October Tom was silent. The air was colder at night and he hated the chill. Every day he returned from school and retreated to his bedroom, wrapping himself in the warm womb of his down sleeping bag. Like a skinny somulent bear, he came out of hibernation only for an occasional meal. And he became cantankerous, arguing about food, clothing, shelter and Mexicans at every opportunity. In contrast, I had energy. I was learning this Mexico City puzzle and I wanted to explore. I gave Tom chances to join me, but he usually responded with an "Uhh, not now," or "I'm to cold," or "Leave me alone."

For two months I had been anxious to explore the underworld of this city. I circled the *PLACES TO LEAVE THE TAXI RUNNING* section in the *AAA* guide book. Those were just the places I wanted to see. Tom wouldn't go, but Squid was game. "Yeah man," he agreed excitedly. "You should have seen those places in Africa. Man with those ivory teeth those native women could really tickle your pecker. Especially the young ones. Man they had some girls who couldn't have been any older than twelve. Let's go."

We went on the night of the Day of the Dead. In Mexico City the peasants prepared to celebrate by the graves of their kin. Food was served and candles were lit on the dirt mounds. Then the lonely dead sojourned back to Mexico for a once-a-year fling at life. They accepted the homage of the unlucky living for one joyous night, leaving them at dawn to their temporal pain and suffering. The families left at first light, abandoning their mystical beauty and nourishment to the appetites of scavenging dogs and satisfying their own immediate hunger with the food of the lesser gods.

We took a pesero taxi to the Avenida Chapultepec and then paid a full fare to the Calle de Los Ninos Periditos, the street of the lost children. Here, there were no street lights. Casket stores occupied the block before the red-light district. The cheap metal caskets reflected the passing shine of occasional car lights like stars appearing from behind moving clouds. The streets were lonely, but a muffled roar of laughter and mariachi music crept through the thin air. From under dark doorways, we saw the pale lights of the whorehouses sliding towards us.

Outside one bar stood a six-foot stuffed ape with red light bulbs blinking where the eyes had once been. His right hand extended a greeting. I knew this was a place I couldn't resist. "This is it, Squid," I decreed. "Cheetah is inviting us inside. I'll bet this place has a homey atmosphere. Why, they probably serve apple pie and ice cream."

"Oh man. All right! I've got twenty bucks." Squid approved, pulling his money out and shoving it into him front pocket. "I'll bet I can get a girl in here for five."

"Or an ape for ten," I calculated.

Inside, we sat at a small metal table near the right wall. On top of the coverless table a golden crown was painted, an advertisement for Brandy Presidente. There was a square bar in the center of the room with large double doors behind it. A juke box was pushed against the left wall and the tables and chairs were cleared to form a small dance floor. Plastic palm trees decorated with Christmas lights were scattered throughout the room. There were no foreigners in the bar. The patrons were working class Mexicans with that Saturday night haircut smell and ill-fitting dress clothes. They were engaging the prostitutes and bartenders in easy conversation and didn't appear to notice us, but the girls did. The prostitutes buzzed and nodded towards us with reserved curiosity. Eventually, one brave employee circled our way. I was afraid of that. She had the build and looks of a penguin. Her bleached-white bosom was slightly covered by a thin black negligee and large pointed lips resembled a beak. She waddled, her hips shifting the fat from side to side and her breasts were lost in folds of skin. Without asking, she ordered a round of brandies by nodding her neckless head towards the bar. Fortunately for me, she sat in Squid's lap. "You hav-a-ah bah-na-nah. You gib mi bah-nan-nah?"

"Oh shit. I don't want this one," Squid wailed desperately. "You speak some Spanish, get rid of her!"

The drinks arrived along with another girl, four brandies in hand. She was a tall black girl who looked like a giraffe. She had a huge butt, small waist, skinny legs and a long neck with a skeleton head. "Hell-o, ow you," she asked in a dignified tone of voice.

"Here's another, take you pick," I offered. Looks like we've got two language majors."

"Oh, God, pick of what," Squid said nervously. "Let's get out of here."

Instantly, afraid they were losing their financial meal, the girls bounced up and pulled us towards the dance floor. "Danza, Danza," the penguin commanded. Now, the entire bar was looking at us. I was afraid that they were looking for an insult. "Just try and desert these Mexican girls, Gringo," they were thinking. "Just try."

"Squid, I think this bunch is waiting to fight a battle with Gringos that's already been fought. You remember, the Alamo. I think we had better danza," I suggested as I shifted my eyes towards the crowd at the bar.

"Yeah, maybe so," he agreed. "Maybe we better get drunk and friendly too."

"Drunk. Barracho!" the Giraffe translated. "Mas Presidente, per favor," she shouted to the bartender. He delivered another round of brandies to our table while we danced.

The girls insisted on slow songs, so they rubbed their bodies against us in no particular rhythm while we sweated to the sonic wail of Mexican love ballads. This was the bump and grind of chaos. We returned to our table for drinks, and then back to the dance floor, Squid and I scanning the crowd for their reactions. Soon, we were getting drunk. "I may be fucked up," Squid said. "But I'm not gonna fuck this beast. We gotta try and escape this cage."

"I've gotta plan," I responded, showing a controlled smile in order to mask my true intentions. "Let's call for the bill and act as if we have money to pay for it. We'll act like we really want these girls and order another round of drinks. We'll go for one last dance and when we pass the door, we'll make a run for it. Otherwise, we're dead meat. Now, let's act more drunk than we really are and show these beauties some attention."

I rubbed the legs of my black giraffe and pretended to stare at her skinny hot-dog tits that hung down like untied shoelaces. Squid kissed his penguin on the cheek and licked her ear. We were both making sacrifices. "We dance," I said, rubbing her cunt and cooing "yo te quiero."

"Uhh, me too," Squid said as he lightly pinched the Penguin's nipples. In all that fat, I don't know how he found them.

The bar seemed at ease. We were showing an interest in their women. It was a matter of honor: the gringos had been conquered. I was experiencing Cortez in the reverse. More brandies arrived with the bill which was over a hundred dollars. I laughed, ordered another round, and pretended to stumble when we got up to dance. I knocked over the drinks and began to chuckle and shake my head, my tongue lolling from my mouth like a bull's. The bar seemed appeased. The gringos were OK. They were spending their Disneyland money on Mexican whores and booze. They would leave nothing, no credit cards here, just cold cash for services rendered and no refunds.

We were lucky. The bouncer was inside and standing a few feet from the door rather than outside on the steps. All we had to do was to escape the bouncer. I knew we could outrun him. Squid and I put our arms around the necks of the prostitutes as we approached our goal. Then I nodded and we bolted out the door, down the steps and toward the Avenida Chapultepec, past the casket stores and up the blocks of darkness. Slowly, the weak glow of street lights rolled into view. Gasping, we stopped at the intersection of the Avenida Chapultepec and Calle de Los Ninos Periditos. There was nobody following us. The dark streets behind us were empty. "God damn," Squid panted. "God damn."

Then I started laughing. I couldn't help it. "This is it Squid. This is living," I yelled. Let's have some music." And I sang *JUST LIKE TOM THUMB'S BLUES:*

> *Well, you're lost in Juarez when it's Easter time too.*
> *And your gravity fails and negativity don't pull you through.*
> *Don't put on any airs when down on Rue Morgue Avenue.*
> *They got some hungry women there and they'll really make a mess out of you.*

We hailed the first taxi and took it all the way home—full fare.

When we arrived Shotgun was stretched out on a bare mattress in front of the fire. She was still, but her eyes were open and without movement. "Shotgun, are you sick," I asked gently as I kneeled down beside her.

"He's going to die," she said. "I know it now. He's going to die. I went back to the prison again today. They have taken his money and put him in a community cell. He's cleaning toilets and he's been raped, me too." I got her a glass of wine. She sipped it while I held her hand. Despite the warmth of the fire, she was stiff and cold. "They wouldn't let me see him alone. I saw him in a visitors room with guards and other prisoners around. Some of them were getting hand jobs from their girls right there in front of everybody. I talked with him for thirty minutes and then three of the guards took me to an empty cell. Each one raped me while the others watched. They told me that they would kill him if I refused. The two who weren't raping me smoked while they watched. They said that if I came back once a week everything would be OK, I figure that at least he'll be alive for a while."

"You can't go back," I pleaded.

"I even had a plan, sort of. I stopped by Tilly's on the way back here. I thought she might have an old nun's habit. She could smuggle in some stuff under it, money, dope, maybe even a weapon so he could escape or at least protect himself. I didn't think the guards would strip a nun. But she said nun's can't wear their habits in public here. And it wouldn't do any good anyway because they would strip a nun, maybe even worse."

"Listen Shotgun, there's nothing you can do alone in the long run. We'll contact the embassy."

"I've tried that before." Shotgun buried her face in her hands, pressuring her temples with her fingers. "They just let drug cases die. We're their bad children. They want us to be punished. We're the prodigal sons and daughters who can't go home."

"You need a doctor?" Squid asked with concern.

"No, I need a priest," she answered. "A very old priest. When

I was a little girl, Father De Fazio, a very old priest with a short white beard, used to take my confessions. He told me that it wasn't so bad to talk back to my parents, shoplift and masturbate, as long as you loved God. Well, I guess that I'm bad, because I don't love God anymore. Now I need to know what he thinks. Is it OK now, not to love God, to love nothing."

"It's OK Shotgun," I replied as I hugged her. "It's OK."

The next morning Shotgun and her belongings were gone.

Within the next few days, Squid redeemed his shipment and traded it at the markets for what he thought was a mountain of turquoise and silver. But when he returned to the house Tom thought it looked suspicious and applied the litmus test of the jeweler: he bit it. His teeth left deep marks in soft plastic-coated plaster. And the silver was mostly tin. Squid left for California dead broke. We loaned him money for gas.

10

Whenever I wanted to be alone, I climbed to our roof and looked to the mountains. Above Mexico City's pollution, Popo and Ixtla dominated the skyline like lonely lighthouses along a flat seashore. After absorbing these mystical volcanoes I felt rinsed out, pure and clean as sun-dried laundry. I was drawn to these mountains, not just to view but to climb and in some way possess. I felt I wanted to be part of their something, whatever it is that drives men to give them the names of legends and worship from their peaks.

The third weekend in November, I went to climb Popo with my guide, Marty, a senior at the American School who had climbed

Popo twenty times. His German father had served in Hitler's Alpine troops and he supplied us with ice-axes and cramp-ons issued originally by the Third Reich.

Tom came along with Angie, a student teacher from Minnesota. He was coming out of his self-imposed exile and once again was joining the world of sinners. Angie was certainly the temptation: long-legged, marine blue eyes and a Jewish princess snootiness made her a very attractive girl. Also, she exhibited an innocent emptiness about this wild country that Tom loved to exploit as her protector and guide.

We approached Popo from the only highway route, a road from the west that led through the ancient village of Ameca-Ameca. This town was a place of lingering time where farmers had tilled the rich volcanic soil for centuries. Some of the best pot in the world came from this area. On this Saturday morning the Indian women sat browning maize patties on their braziers and vendors hocked their wares from blankets spread on the pavement. Popo dominated the east, turning a deep blue directionless sky into a two dimensional portrait, and Ixtla rolled off to the north.

As the four of us breezed through the market, I noticed one unusual exhibit, the mountaineers' display. There were boots, some pairs almost new, cramp-ons, polished and sharp, down coats, some slightly torn and many other necessities of the sport.

"What about it Marty?" I asked. "I can buy my own equipment for a song here."

"I wish I hadn't seen this stuff," he answered. "It's cursed."

"Bad luck?" I questioned.

"Yeah, this stuff came off dead bodies," he replied. "The ones who died on the mountains. You can get it real cheap because nobody wants it."

"Walk a mile in my shoes," Tom sang as he fingered a used pair of Dunlap boots.

"Very funny," Angie giggled, punching him on the shoulder. "Don't make fun of a ghost or they'll get us. You told me that around here the dead still live."

"The ghosts won't get us sweetheart," Tom said lightheartedly. "They're the ones who are going to try and climb the mountain. He pointed a finger of warning at Marty and me. "We're going to stay by a warm fire and cheer them on to victory."

Leaving Ameca-Ameca, we traveled the well-paved road that delivered us to the lodge at twelve-thousand feet. The lodge had a large circular fireplace in a central room. Most of the southern wall was a picture window that framed the northern Las Cruzes route of the mountain. Outside the window was a telescope for viewing the climbers' progress. The lodge also had a large kitchen with many gas grills and a sleeping section with six small rooms containing four bunkbeds per room. There wasn't much privacy, except with your own thoughts.

After studying the mountain, Marty decided we would ascend by the western El Castillo route, so named for a large pile of boulders that resembled a castle at about fifteen-thousand feet, and to descend the mountain by the traditional Las Cruzes route.

"Don't worry," Marty assured me. "El Castillo is a more difficult route, but it's more spectacular. We've got the proper equipment and I've got the knowledge and experience. Just play follow the leader."

I wasn't scared. I was determined. I wanted to own that mountain and bind my past failures into the crater's roaring fury. I wanted to take from it what I thought I needed.

Marty gave me a quick survival course in mountaineering. He instructed me how to use a safety rope and ice-ax and how to break a fall by putting my weight on the ax and driving it into the snow. "That's all you need to know for this climb" he concluded. "Now you can protect yourself and your partner when you fall."

Tom and Angie slept in the lodge, but Marty and I decided to sleep outside in our sleeping bags facing the mountains. Before I slept, I inhaled the stars myriad lights as they illuminated Popo's snow. I saw better at night than I did during the day. Vivid shadows were clearer at night, like dreams the instant before waking. I stared at the mountain for hours before I slept, waiting for it to solidify my life's jumble before I waked.

We began our ascent at 3:30 A.M. The first two hours were a walk up the soft volcanic dirt. I couldn't help but think this soil was the compost of the Cortez myth. His men had walked it to gather sulfur for the gunpowder assault on Tenochtitlán. We reached the path that led through Popo's western rocky area in time to see the sunrise off Ixtla's breast to the north. Softly, Ixtla seemed to absorb the early light. I took a quick shot of Fundador with my ham sandwich breakfast and washed it down with the ice-cold water from my canteen. This was it, the way I wanted things, escaping towards the top, and pausing before the temporary grasp of eternity.

"The path's pretty good for the next couple of hours until we reach castle rock," Marty observed. "Getting tired?"

"No", I answered abruptly. "This is incredible. I never felt so fucking good in my whole life. How high are we now?"

"Oh, about fourteen-thousand feet. It'll get tougher, the altitude I mean. You may feel sick. Let me know if you do. Altitude sickness can be serious. If it happens, we'll have to get you down."

"Ha, no way," I shouted, the sound carrying in the empty air. "I'm not surrendering to the shit-breathing world below. It's conquer or die."

"If you get sick, we go down," Mary repeated with his German seriousness. "There's more than just you involved here."

The path to Castle rock was narrow and broken in places by rock piles and boulders, but it was passable by taking turns anchoring each other with a rope, or belaying. We reached the formation at 8:00 A.M. and continued on to a small emergency shelter about a hundred feet above it. Here, we took a cheese and crackers break. The snow line began at the shelter and we squeezed on our crampons for security. About fifty feet east of the shelter was a narrow rock bridge that connected this solitary western section of the mountain to the symmetrical whole. Above this bridge was a two-thousand foot snowfield that led to the peak. About a mile below lay the Valle de Cortez.

"We'll belay each other across the bridge," Marty commanded. "It shouldn't be a problem. We'll be safe."

First, I belayed Marty. He checked the footing as he slowly crossed the bridge to the slope. I tied the safety rope to my ice ax and then to myself, driving the pointed butt of the ax as deeply as I could in the snow and then, from a kneeling position, pressing my full weight on its flat top. "It's solid," he called. "There's not even any ice patches. Your turn." I tied the rope in a figure eight knot around my waist and started across the bridge. "Don't look down," he yelled. I watched my footing but averted my eyes from the steep drop. "Look out," he shouted. I shot my eyes quickly toward him and saw his face frozen toward the south. Still on the bridge, I fell on my ice-ax just as a enormous dark bird cruised over me heading north. It turned sharply and disappeared behind the western rocks. Shaken, I scrambled to my feet and continued my trek toward the snowfield.

"That damn thing almost hit you. I've never seen anything like it. What was it?" Marty huffed, his stoic composure broken.

"I don't know," I gasped. "Perhaps an eagle."

"I've heard that condors have been seen on some mountains in the Sierra Madre. I'll bet that's what it was, but I thought they were almost extinct."

"They are. But I think we just found him. The last of a dying breed."

Carefully, we began ascending. I kept my ice-ax in a fall position with the sharp end behind me so it would be in the proper position to receive my weight if I fell. The slope could be called easy by professional mountaineering standards, but the forty-five degree angle and the high altitude created a treacherous climb, and many men had died on Popo by taking its primitive simplicity for granted.

We criss-crossed up the snowfield, keeping our bodies at near-right angles to the valley far below. By 9:30 A.M., we were halfway up this final challenge and about a thousand feet from the crater. By this time, we had to rest every twenty steps. Even through my dark glacier glasses I squinted against the sun, brighter than even the reflected light of a Florida beach. At this oxygen-poor altitude of over seventeen-thousand feet, my chest heaved like an asmatic's during a severe attack. Several times I had to drop to one knee as spots exploded in my vision like Fourth-of-July fireworks. Suddenly, I saw Marty disappear over the crater's lip. I crawled the last few feet and stumbled to my goal. I was there. I sensed my original ball of clay had suddenly grown beyond its limbs. I had sculptured myself anew, made myself part of this volcano with its ancient ash and steam. I knew I would never return to that land of zombies, that land of time's warp, that other America. Yet, I couldn't let go all of it. There was still something there. I turned to the north and looked toward the good ole USA while the Steve Miller Band flashed its rhetorical refrain through my silence:

Where are you going to, what are you going to do,
Do you think that it was be pleasing...
Smell freedom, don't worry about me babe,
Gotta be free babe, Living in the U.S.A.
Datavision, television politicians, morticians,
Living in the USA.

Then I turned and looked down into the Valle de Cortez, the valley that held the blood and guts of our Western history, but now it held the pot that fed America. Cortez didn't feel so heroic anymore. In fact, he felt awfully small, along with my other heros. I didn't feel any exhilaration, pride, bravado or even happiness I didn't feel anything. I turned to the ocean sky and was absorbed. Now, I understood why ancient people had worshipped on mountains and why altars were the architecture of high places. On a mountain every man became a high priest and communicated with the God before time, the womb of being.

We shared wine cheese and crackers for lunch. I was nauseous because of the sulfur smell from the crater. About a hundred feet down I saw water boiling and gurgling. Concentric rings of snow began at the cold of the crater's lip and spiraled downward until the hot steam met the bottoms of waiting rocks.

"Time to go," Marty stated casually after about an hour's stay. It was past noon. "Let's walk around the rim and descend on the Las Cruzes route."

We were not alone. On the northeast perimeter of the crater were three other climbers. They were taking photographs and laughing. They were dressed in fashionable one-piece blue down jumpsuits with red stripes down the sides and PIKES PEAK CLIMBING CLUB emblazoned across the backs. Marty noticed they didn't have a rope.

"Hey," Marty yelled against the increasing north wind. "You want to share our rope for the descent."

"No thank you," one of them yelled back. "It was an easy climb, a walk-up."

Our eyes scanned the route. Near the crater, the slope was sheer ice. We could see the steps those climbers cut to create their own stairs to the top. The descent would be dangerous but with the clouds we saw approaching, it would be safer than trying El Castillo. If they rolled in before we reached the bridge, we might not be able to find it. "Well, I tried," Marty said with a shrug, turning from the other climbers.

We roped up and began our descent down the mile-long slope. It was less precipitous than the El Castillo route, but an unbroken north wind, warming daytime temperatures and the high altitude sun had created an icy nightmare. Like feeble old men with canes, we descended carefully and slowly, checking our steps with the points of our ice-axes. "We'll stay close to those rocks," Marty commanded as he led us toward a long series of small boulders and gravel that jutted out like a finger about a thousand feet down the mountain. "If we slip, they will break our fall."

After we descended about a hundred feet, we turned and checked on the other climbers. Marty pointed toward the rocks to emphasize our safer route. None of them were paying attention. They were about fifty feet away from the rocks and were beginning their descent. One took a few steps off the rim and then turned to face another climber who was attempting to take his picture. The photographer apparently couldn't get the shot he wanted, so he took a step down and to his right and slipped. Without his ice ax or a rope to slow his fall, he quickly began to slide and then roll. He passed about ten feet from us, his camera still in his hand, teeth gritted, clawing at the hard ice of the unyielding slope. Marty, in a heroic attempt to break his fall, dove at him but missed. The climber began to tumble, bouncing down the mountain. He hit the rocks and cartwheeled into the thin air over the valley.

His companions stood in shock just a step from the rim. Marty shook our rope and motioned that we could ascend and assist them. The two remaining climbers shook their head . They didn't budge. Like two specks of dirt on an ice-cream cone, they hunched over their ice-axes with the points sticking precariously in the mountain. We didn't have time to argue. A large weather front, a norte, was moving in quickly. We had to descend immediately. All I could concentrate on was my own survival. What had started as an enjoyable climb had turned into a death march.

Below the descent became easier. The ice gave way to a thin crunch layer of snow, enough for our cramp-ons to grip, and the angle wasn't as steep. We no longer needed the safety rope. We were going to make it. By 3:30 we were almost at the lodge. We stopped to catch our breath and release our controlled panic. Behind us the mountain was hidden in swirling clouds. "Don't say anything about this," Marty cautioned. "They weren't with us. The police might try to blame us for their deaths."

"But two are still up there," I argued.

"They probably won't get down," Marty said. "I think they want a rescue squad to save them, the National Park Service helicopter or something. But this is Mexico, not fucking Colorado. We only have recovery squads. Those climbers will probably freeze to death or try to descend during the storm and fail. Either way, let's leave in a hurry and not say anything to anybody. Nobody knows us up here. If we're lucky some astronomer wasn't looking through the telescope when he fell."

Tom and Angie were waiting outside by the van when we arrived at the parking lot. "I saw somebody fall through the telescope," Tom whispered. I could see the worry lines on his face. "What the hell happened up there."

We bought a case of Bohemias in Ameca-Ameca and I told the story. Somehow it didn't come out the way I wanted. There was something else I couldn't tell. It just wouldn't come out but I heard the other words, the real words inside me, conversing in the language of ghosts.

"It's you men," Angie challenged brazenly when I finished. "You're drawn toward your egos. It's what you want, to feel immortal."

"And what were you drawn toward Miss Analyst?" I retorted angrily. "Making love while you watched men squirm and die in your telescope, a little death, up close and personal."

Angie lit up a joint and turned toward the passing scenery outside the window. "What do you think, Tom?"

"Not much. The man climbed a mountain and we made love. Men died and they don't concern us. We're OK. Leave it alone."

Angie turned from the window and leaned against Tom's shoulder "You're right," she said.

We became quiet. Soon, I saw the silhouettes of their dark heads against the lights of Mexico City.

11

D ecember in Mexico City is cool and dry. The fall atmosphere
of death, so prevalent in the Day of the Dead season,
surrendered to the gaiety of Christmas and hope of
redemption. Beggars, ageless but old in the soul, shook their black
piggy banks at us during our frequent Zona Rosa visits. I waited for
them to tell my future in biblical riddles.

Angie, Tom and I sat drinking pitchers of Cerveza de Barril in
Happy's Pizza, an American style pizza joint in Techamelchaloco,
a suburb close to our house.

Tom and I finally succumbed to the Colonel's suggestion that
we go to Happy's and find its owner, McNapp, the man he had told
us about several times. McNapp was a nervous-eyed, sandy-haired
Aussie who looked like a well-groomed Willie Nelson. Our first night
there he seemed to recognize us and he welcomed us as if we were
long-lost family.

"The Colonel told us about this place," Tom said to him. "He said
to stop by."

"He did, did he," McNapp said, glancing toward the entrance
in search of potential customers. "Well, he told you right. He knows
I like God-fearing Americans. It's a break from these Mexican
bastards."

On this first visit, McNapp sat and talked with us for hours. In
a friendly way he asked us about our backgrounds, paying special
attention to me and Tom. "What brings you to this hell-hole mates?
And how are your jobs at the American School?"

We were more than willing to talk. We loved it and we filled
his ears with nostalgic Hallmark card reminiscences of homes and
families. And we told him how we loved this naked guts country
and city with its struggling march of survival. Soon we felt clean
as new snow, as if our emotional imaginative confessions helped to

create new intricate flake patterns, and our lives took on momentary meaning.

McNapp also talked to us, or rather complained. "Damned business. Ya can't trust anybody these days. If I leave my God damn employees alone a minute they'll steal me blind. I can't fire the sons-of-bitches because Mexican law won't let me. What a fuckin' country. I can't even find an honest manager for my other store in Zona Rosa. When I'm here they steal from me there, and when I'm there, they steal from me here. I haven't had a vacation in five years. Sons-of-bitches!"

"McNapp, you're clearly a frustrated business man," Tom analyzed. "Why I'll bet the Colonel sent us here to calm you down a little. Hell, money ain't' worth that much. You're gonna be dead before you get a vacation at this rate."

"Yeah, maybe I'll sell out next year, retire to Cuenervaca where I have some friends," McNapp sighed, fluttering his eyelids, a nervous habit that gave him the appearance of a middle-aged homosexual flirting with his young prey.

"Why not start out slow McNapp," I suggested. Come with us to the Guadelope celebrations next Sunday. "We'll take you on a guided culture tour. We'll hit the market and the bullfights. Maybe we'll start early and visit the shrine and watch the peasants crawl to the church and pray to that cloth with Mary's polaroid snapshot on it."

"You mean the cloth that she supposedly gave that stupid Indian back in the 1500's?" McNapp appeared interested. "I was in a similar business when I first came to Mexico. I opened a factory in Valle de Bravo that made doormats stamped with the names of American baseball teams. I employed over two-hundred peasants and I sold it for a million dollars. God told me to do it. He's a Yankee fan."

"Then come with us McNapp," Angie pleaded. "And bring your girlfriend."

"I've got a wife," he replied sternly. "She's in Europe."

Sunday, the beginning of the third week in December, is the day of celebration for the miracle of Guadelope. During this week in 1533, Juan Lopez, an illiterate Indian peasant and a survivor of the Cortez Apocalypse, claimed a visitation from the Virgin Mary while on his way to Mexico City. He went straight to the bishop and told his story. Naturally, the good bishop didn't believe him. So the Blessed Virgin appeared to Juan a second time and gave him a mantle to deliver to the doubting bishop. Juan returned, and when he presented this souvenir to his Holy Reverent, an image of her was imprinted in the cloth. Now, for centuries millions of peasant pilgrims have sojourned to her shrine at the Guadelope Church to thank their holy patroness for the visitation. By tradition, they crawl on their knees for miles to do penance for their sins before her image. Bloodied by the hard concrete and harassed by irritated motorists, they at last receive absolution.

We arrived at the unimposing gray church in early morning. This ugly structure more like concrete than brick, seemed like apostasy. The area around the church was so packed with peasants I couldn't see the ground. This mob was babbling in ancient tongues as it crawled slowly toward the steps and door that led to the mystical maiden's shrine.

"My God," Angie shuddered. "They look like a swarm of insects. It even sounds as if they're buzzing."

"What the hell are they muttering about?" McNapp asked.

"They're praying, McNapp," I answered.

"Why?" he asked. "Look at the poor, ragged, bloody sons-of-bitches. Just what the hell do they think they're going to get."

"Maybe a job at Happy's Pizza," Tom chuckled.

One Indian woman, old and creased as a spoiled vegetable, stopped her crawl at the top step. She crumbled into a heap like dirty laundry and disappeared into her dirty gray shawl.

"Shit, I think she's dead," Tom whispered.

The mob didn't stop. Like soldiers retreating across no man's land over bodies of enemy soldiers, it scooted over her toward salvation.

"She may have just fainted," Angie said hopefully.

"Even so," I observed. "She'll probably be dead soon with this crowd rolling over her."

"We can't help?" Tom pleaded. His eyes had the yellowish look of someone about to vomit.

"Get used to it, Tom," McNapp said. "This is National Geographic on its day off."

McNapp was impressed with La Laguanilla. He scavenged through the junk stands like an alley cat, turning over piles until he hit bottom. "They stole this stuff, huh mate," he asked rhetorically.

"Some of it," I answered. "You look surprised. Haven't you been to a thieves market before?"

"No mate," he responded jovially. "I avoid these kind of people as much as possible. They're only any good if they make you money. But I have to admit, they are entertaining."

"So McNapp," I continued. "If you hate these Mexicans so much why do you stay here?" You've made your money. Why don't you go home to Australia?"

"I've been here too long mate," he answered. I've got responsibilities here that have nothing to do with the Mexicans. I can't leave now. I guess you wonder how I landed here in the first place?"

"Not really," I answered. "You told me you started a business." McNapp and I were alone. The others were watching Tom bargain for a mask.

"I won a gold medal in the 1960 Summer Olympics," McNapp began as he fingered some silverware at a stand. He ignored my brush off. "I was an equestrian representing my country, Australia. During the games, I fell in love with a Mexican girl who rode for Mexico. God mate, was she a dark beauty. She looked like Elizabeth Taylor with dark skin. Three months after the games we married and I moved to her family's ranch in the Michucan province. I became head trainer at their stables which included prize race horses. She divorced me after a few years, but I had made some money connections and stayed. Eventually, I took advantage of my opportunities. Isn't that the way you yanks do it?"

I was curious why McNapp had chosen me for this confidence instead of making conversation over a few beers at Happy's. He seemed intent on crumbling his private history out in tidbits, like a three year old eating animal crackers.

Meanwhile, Tom bought a mask of a rabbit's face covered in fur. When he modeled the mask he looked like some child's nightmare of the Easter Bunny. Angie bought an antique hair clasp and a hand-painted vase. I bought a Mexican army belt buckle, but McNapp found nothing, his story was enough.

"You know that scene on Keat's Grecian urn where the lovers are about to kiss?" Angie asked Tom. "Well, the nymphs on this vase remind me of them and their message: people live in a perpetual state of horniness. Maybe I'll just rub this thing and my own genie will pop out. I'll ask for the world's three best lovers and then I won't need you anymore Tom."

"So that's all it is." Tom shook his head in mock disappointment. "I thought you wanted my soul."

"Oh, I'll get that anyway," Angie said as she grabbed Tom's hand and led him to the van for a joint.

The Guadelope celebrations promised the best corridas of the season. Officially, this was the first day of the professional season in Mexico. The main attraction was Manolo Martinez, currently the most popular matador, noted for his reckless courage and willingness to fight the bulls close. Also, Hector Rodriguez, the young novillero who Tom and me had seen in September, was scheduled to take his alternative on this holy day. I had bought tickets well in advance in the barrera seats on the third row in the sun. It was shining hard on this day and we drank several Coronas waiting for four o'clock. Angie was stoned and appeared to be studying the crowd, but her blank expression betrayed her true condition. McNapp was enjoying himself. He listened intently while I explained the drama to him.

After the opening ceremonies, Manolo Martinez presented the young Rodriguez with his muleta and sword. The matador took the place of the older one for the first corrida of the day. It was his professional initiation. The older matador moved to second in the order.

Hector Rodriguez's bull charged fast and its horn thrust was straight. The young matador waved off his assistants and after some preliminary passes executed three beautiful Veronicas that wiped the tears off the Savior's eyes. The crowd stood and shouted "Oles" in unison to the final Veronica. It was an excellent beginning.

The picadores and banderilleros captured the excitement of this new matador's moment and prepared the bull like a feast. It still had spirit and they didn't want it broken. Hector Rodriguez began the final act with the difficult ayudado por alto pass, lifting the muleta over the bull's head and passing him underneath it. Rodriguez was still as a sculpture. It was this deceptive stillness that gave his performance such emotion. Then, he led his bull into three full naturals that appeared to halt time with each movement a different still frame. In the dull gray light of the fading afternoon, these pictures were surreal, an anachronism haunting the present. Now, it was time to kill.

His estocada was splendid as his lean body arched over the bull's horns and his right arm thrust the sword into the soft spot in the bull's back that led to his heart. The bull fell like carelessly unloaded freight, the final shove of emotion. Thousands of white handkerchiefs waved in the crowd. Hector Rodriguez was awarded two ears and a tail. Later this evening, this toro's cojones would be served as a delicacy at a local restaurant.

Manolo Martinez followed the newly crowned matador. He wasn't handsome; his short bow-legs exploded below a squat torso;

hair, flat as paper, was plastered to the top of his small Indian head; his traje de luces looked like a traffic light stuck on green; and his color was dark. He seemed stiff, his troll body contorted with the voyeuristic tension of his young rival's success. This was no longer a festival: it was a competition.

Tom rested his chin on his hands and watched. He had a feel for significant moments. I know he identified with Manolo Martinez, the old, popular matador still trying to justify his appeal. Tom was only twenty-eight, but to Angie, the child whose lovers were playmates and whose feelings were immediate, he was old. I sensed Tom was slipping out of his time. He was spreading his cape for the last natural that would spin him from his corrida into the void of certainty. I wasn't sure he would go smoothly.

The picadores spiked the huge brown bull deep in the neck muscle several times. Blood spread like paint over the bull's sides. Manolo Martinez placed the banderillas himself to a chorus of "Oles" from the crowd. After the third set was placed, he turned to the crowd to show the tattered rip across the stomach of his traje de Luces. He had led the bull to the third act of the tragedy.

During the faena, Manolo Martinez dominated, wrapping the bull around him several times with naturals. But he was also crude, making crowd-pleasing passes from his knees and once turning his back to the bull and rotating at the last second for the pass. He reminded me more of a clown at a rodeo than an artistic matador. He broke his rhythm attempting to win the crowd from Hector Rodriguez. Most of the crowd loved it, but the bull was left confused, hesitant and dangerous.

"The bull's going into his querencia," I explained to Angie and McNapp. "That's the small area of space around him where he feels most secure. Earlier, he charged hard because he felt the instinct of home. But now, you see, he's given up going home and he's found a place to defend. He's very dangerous there."

"We're all dangerous there," McNapp said.

Manolo Martinez made a mistake when he decided to kill the bull rather than trying to take him out of the querencia with more passes. He didn't want to risk failure. He took the sword in his right hand, dropped the capate low with his left hand and lunged over the bull's horns. The sword bent and leaped into the air as if it had a life of its own. Again he tried with the same result.

Angie wasn't watching this struggle. She giggled and laughed while she pointed out to Tom events in the crowd: two drunks fighting, outrageously dressed ladies and the reactions of a disgusted tourist.

"Bloody bastards love this sort of thing," McNapp commented, gesturing wildly towards the crowd behind us. "Maybe I'll start another factory that puts matadors on welcome mats. Hell mates, just come on in and we'll stick a sword in ya." But despite his humorous complaints, McNapp was an observer. Like an old time pilot checking the ocean, he studied this human sea for every detail. I watched him and I wasn't sure if his study was for enjoyment or something that I couldn't name. He hadn't seemed to enjoy much since I had known him.

The Mexicans began to whistle their disapproval at Manolo Martinez's performance. A few cushions sprinkled into the arena. He aimed his sword and went over the bull's horns, but just as he leaned over them a cushion landed at his feet. I could see his eyes momentarily flick towards this gutless object as he tripped and landed on the bull's rising head. The left horn tore into his exposed groin severing the femoral artery, a matador's achilles heel. He was never thrown. The angry bull nailed him into the sand like an angry carpenter pounding a recalcitrant nail. It took five minutes for his fellow matadors to distract the bull away. He was quickly dragged toward the infirmary, leaving uneven spots of sandy blood in his wake. The next day the newspapers ran close-up pictures of his death.

"My God, the bull won," Tom exclaimed. "Damn, I hear these tourists say all the time that they wish the bull would win but you don't expect it to happen. It's different, like the destruction of a painting or a sculpture."

I thought of Goya and how he captured the messy spectacle of bullfights and turned them into something enduring and beyond the moment. Manolo Martinez wouldn't be in a Goya painting. He would be dead and the crowd would go home, get drunk, fuck their wives, husbands, sweethearts and nobodies, and then sleep, get up and face another day without moments.

"What did he do wrong?" Angie asked. "Did he try to make it too pretty?"

"He tried to go beyond art," I explained. "He entered the twilight zone."

"It was pride," Tom said. "He didn't want that youngster to upstage him. He had to do it and go on. He couldn't lose his place."

"Bullshit," McNapp snickered. "Dumb son-of-a-bitch got what he deserved. After all, what's another dead spic. But he was entertaining, I'll give him that much. I wish that it had'uv happened to that pretty-boy matador that my ex-wife ran off with. I think he got smart and quit after he got her. Went to breeding bulls I hear."

I didn't feel like arguing with McNapp and neither did anyone else. We were all in our own emotional caskets. I could sense that chilling kinship with death we all felt. But it wasn't a proximity to death that bothered me anymore I was growing accustomed to its everyday nearness. It swelled over this city like a thunderhead. What bothered me was what it left behind: the drowned finality of the present, our sloshing daily through the streets like drunken beggars toward our resolutions.

For us, the Corrida de Toros had ended. We left for Happy's Pizza where his country music juke-box entertained us with Hank Williams's *COLD COLD HEART.*

12

We all decided to stay in Mexico for Christmas and used our vacation time to travel to Taxco, Cuernevaca, Toluca and other central Mexican attractions. Tom and Angie loved to spend hours haggling with the merchants over special wares. In Taxco they bought Spalding silver and in Toluca wool blankets, woven so tightly that a pin couldn't be stuck through them. Their shopping began to acquire a domestic quality. Tom acted like a jealous high school boyfriend, arguing with Angie over her mention of any old boyfriends about anything in her life before they met. She knew it and selectively used her control. Before long, Tom was talking romantically about marrying Angie in the Pueblo Cathedral, one of the most beautiful in all of Mexico. She had no comment.

Sometimes on these trips I brought Margarita along for entertainment. She prowled through the most expensive items and made a show of bargaining with the seller. Then she replaced the items and sneered, more at its quality than at its price which, she couldn't afford. Sometimes, I think she thought I was going to buy it for her. That was the Disneyland approach to shopping. All Americans are rich and he's an American and I know it and so does the merchant but we don't need your junk because we've got the money to buy something better. And besides, here's one in your face. Who's got Texas now! From the merchants I got tight-lipped stares. They knew Margarita was a peasant and I was stealing their woman. Some future Mexican mother was in my bed, another American victory.

McNapp came with us to Taxco. He wanted to buy something for his wife's Christmas present, even though she wouldn't return to Mexico until Spring. We thought his relationship with his wife was odd. They spent many months apart and McNapp didn't appear to miss her. Actually, he spent more memories on his first wife, the one who left him for the matador. And we never ask him about his personal life. That was his business. But he would volunteer bolts of information suddenly and always to only one of us. After three weeks, we all knew his history. Interestingly, it was the same story, a mantra recited to different people at different times.

In Taxco, he spent most of his time in the silver shops. Finally, he bought an elaborate bejeweled necklace for two-thousand dollars. "I don't think she'll like it mates, if she finds out that it's so cheap," he said. "Don't tell her."

Despite our attempts to relax McNapp, he complained about Happy's Pizza all the way back to Mexico City. "I'm going to sell out. Hell, I might give it away," he griped, his eyebrows furrowed and his Aussie accent as harsh as sandpaper. "I'm just putting up with this for friends anyway. Hell, my wife's an heiress with a family fortune. I shouldn't have anything to worry about. It's time to cash in on some favors. Fuck'um."

"Fuck who McNapp," Angie asked.

"Them," McNapp replied angrily. "The whole damn group. I have to put up with too much shit from people. I ought to be like you and not have to worry about anything. You don't know nobody and nobody knows you."

"So, move to the states," I suggested. "It can't be as bad there."

"Hell, it's worse," McNapp countered. "Besides, I got in a spot of trouble there once. Legally, I can't get back in. Technicalities, you know."

No one questioned McNapp's revelations. It was part of our rambler's creed that we didn't fly into someone's past. He was feeding us pieces of his history like birdseed, but we never pecked his hand. He was our friend now and he would divulge himself in due time if he wished. Tom and I didn't want to play emotional martyrs, the saints of other peoples' problems. We wanted to be priest of the present.

Tom shoved the Mexican's favorite, Credance Clearwater Revival, in the cassette:

Lookin' for a job in the city, working for the man
every night and day.
But I never lost a minute of sleepin worrin bout
the way things might have been.
Big wheels keep on movin, Proud Mary keeps on movin.
Rollin, Rollin, Rollin on the river...

"Fucking noise makes me want to puke," McNapp groaned. "I hadn't liked anything since Frank Sinatra."

On Christmas Eve night we held a party at our place. McNapp provided pizza appetizers and Tilly cooked a turkey. It was a small group. Ramon, Tilly's boyfriend, was with her. Margarita was with me, Angie and Tom were together and John Coles stopped by for a few minutes of Christmas cheer.

Except for big John Coles, who brought a case of Bohemia beer, we all had packages either to wrap or unwrap. Several weeks before, I had carefully mailed my mother eight ruby crystal glasses. I had saved her package and letter until tonight. I had written her faithfully every week, but it was usually just postcards that read "Hi, how are you and how's the weather" stuff. I wouldn't admit it, but I was too busy for more writing. Phone calls were easier. Her letters to me weren't long but they were filled with concern and the tension of uncertainty about my safety. I was an only child. I don't think she enjoyed the phone calls, her voice often broke. I avoided topics such as mountain climbing and Margarita and concentrated mostly on tourist sites and school. I never even told her I missed her.

Tom was the most anxious about his loved ones. "Damn, I really should have gone home this Christmas. You know I've missed the last three," he said, moving the Christmas package around in his hands like an archeologist examining an artifact. "I mean, my old man is nuts and I know he can't take care of her."

"Oh hell, what could you do," McNapp said, spearing another piece of turkey and plopping it down in his plate.

"You don't know my dad. He lost most of his retirement in an attempt to smuggle truckloads of bananas in from Honduras. We never did find out what happened to the bananas. They disappeared."

"Bananas. There's no money in that," McNapp pointed out.

"Probably not, but that's dear old dad. Now, he's growing marijuana in the house. There's clay pots in every window sill."

"I can see why you want to go home," Tilly said. It sounds like your mother could use your help. She pushed through the kitchen door with a pan of fresh rolls.

"Shut up, you're making me feel guilty," John Coles said. "I ought to be home now, my Mexican home that is. Pass some of those rolls over here."

"If you miss home so much then what keeps you here?" Tilly asked.

"I don't know. I think my mother knows. I know that living in Montgomery works for a while, and then I feel like I've got to go, like I'm confined. Anyway I get along better with the family long distance. That's all I guess."

"I know the feeling, being confined," Tilly said, serving herself for the first time. "Sometimes you can do more on your own, for everyone I mean. She patted Ramon on the shoulder. "Isn't that right matador?" Because of McNapp, I was worried when Tilly told me she was bringing him. But McNapp wasn't bothered. He didn't appear to have anything against matadors in general, at least no more than he had against all Mexicans.

"I know you do much for me. Maybe soon I will give up the bulls for other things. Merry Christmas." Ramon proposed a toast to us, his host and another to Tilly, the best critic of his poetry.

There was a Christmas tree, cut in the mountains around Toluca, decorated with popcorn strings, candy canes and little wire figures Tom made of Santa and the reindeer. Carlota, her feathers the colors of the holiday, added to the trimmings by perching in our rubber plant. McNapp played Santa and handed out the gifts. My mother sent me three flannel shirts and a London Fog jacket; Tom's mother sent a retouched antique picture of herself and Tom's father in a wooden frame; Angie's parents sent her five hundred dollars; and Tilly's sister sent a summer plane ticket for Paris. McNapp didn't have a gift from his wife. "She'll bring it with her when she comes," he explained, after he passed out the last gifts. We don't really care for this sort of thing ya know. Holidays and all that."

Except for the couples, we didn't exchange gifts among ourselves. Angie and I pooled our money and bought Tom a deer mask; Tom bought Angie a silver charm bracelet with an assortment of Mexican turquoise animal figurines to start her collection; Tilly gave Ramon a collection of Shakespeare's sonnets; and I gave Margarita mother-of-pearl earrings, large multicolored crosses that dangled from her ears by thick, gold chains. I hoped that like most Mexicans, prostitute or not, she was Catholic, or at least Christian. I hadn't put much thought into the gift. I got them near the Cathedral at one of the hundreds of pawn shops on the Zocalo's periphery. "Oh, John, John," she moaned, hugging my neck with her strong hands. "Gracias mi amor." I was a little embarrassed by her affections. Tilly gave me a slight shake of the head and turned her attention towards the Sonnets, flipping through the pages to show Ramon her favorites. Angie laughed, drawing a menacing look from Margarita.

After the tree ceremony, we passed around Christmas joints and several bottles of French Burgundy Tilly had brought. Tilly and Ramon refused the joint but didn't seem to mind our indulgence. Margarita angrily waved it off and glared suspiciously at Angie, as if she were the corruptor. "So Angie, are you staying here for the new year?" Tilly asked.

"I think so, at least for a while," Angie answered. I'm going to substitute at the school. There's a good chance a few positions will open up next year and I would like one of them."

"Yes, positions always open up, people leave, suddenly sometimes if their situations deteriorate."

"You mean when the women get tired of their husbands taking lovers and flaunting their machoism." Angie glanced at Ramon.

"Yes, sometimes that's it." Tilly took a sip of wine, barely wetting her lips.

"That's the Latin way, isn't it."

"Not for all of us," John Coles corrected. I don't run around on my wife."

"The women here have more respect," Ramon passed the joint to Angie. "They are the mothers of our children. We have an obligation to them."

"That's nice. That's real nice." Angie inhaled. "Isn't that nice Tom?"

"I don't know. Why don't you ask Margarita here. Get the woman's opinion."

"I don't believe her opinion applies to us," Tilly said.

"Que, Que?" asked Margarita.

"Es poco importante?" I answered, hoping to halt Angie's argument. "So Ramon, you're quite a combination, a matador and a poet. What's the connection?"

"The matador and the poet both create and destroy." Ramon turned the pages of sonnets slowly, as if he were looking for one that would help him.

"How's that?" Tom asked.

"Every time I write a poem I destroy a feeling, so it can be replaced by another." Ramon took a long drink of wine, placed his arms on his knees and fixed his reply on Angie. "And every time I fight a bull, I create and then destroy, so there could be another creation. Comprende?"

"Is the next creation better or worse?" I asked.

"Always better."

"So destruction means creation," Angie summarized, taking another hit of the joint she had just rolled. She passed it to McNapp and he took it. "You know I kind of like that." Carlota hopped down from her perch and waddled to Angie, eating the birdseed she offered from the palm of her hand.

"Oh shit, this is pot talk," John Coles said as he got up to leave. I've gotta get on home to the wife and child. But I enjoyed it. Merry Christmas everybody."

"John's right," Tilly said, placing Ramon's hand on hers. "Let's drop the philosophy. It's Christmas."

"I propose a toast." I raised my glass. "To the family we have here in this room, Merry Christmas and a Happy New Year. Salud!"

And Margarita was never better than that night, her earrings jangling on my pillow.

Jingle Bells, Jingle Bells,
Jingle all the way.

13

L ate winter in Mexico City is the dry season. Days are windy and dusty and nights are clear and still with a zero-bone chill. These nights I often found myself alone reading. I had finished Bernal del Castillo and was through studying history for a while. Instead, I became more interested in novels. I felt more at home delving into characters' lives and seeing how the graves of their personalities were uncovered a fistful of soil at a time. Instead of external events, I was obsessed with internal connections, the motivations. I read *UNDER THE VOLCANOES* in front of the fireplace and I couldn't help thinking about my partner in that book:

that pathetic hero driving his alcoholic ambulance into the grave. It bothered me that he seemed to want to go. He knew the route with shortcuts and he went there with a long siren. I didn't want to follow him.

Tom and Angie avoided me. I knew I was being severed like an unwanted wart from their lives. I avoided them. When we unavoidably collided, Angie, like an angry bird protecting her nest, attacked my whole being, but I was mute to her screeches. She told me my increasing passion for mountaineering was an "egotistical mania," and she accused me of debasing woman by "taking up with that stupid whore Margarita." Margarita sensed her anger and stayed away.

Angie was battling me for control. To possess Tom and take him out of his world, she had to eliminate me. She had to envelope Tom's life and send it registered mail to herself. I was surprised and hurt at how easily Tom let himself be signed, sealed and delivered.

I wandered the streets alone and rode the metro. My car was dead, a victim of altitude breakdown and Mexican import laws: I couldn't get the parts to fix it. But I enjoyed the metro, the caravan of the poor. Despite the crush of people I could get a good lonely feeling here. I could turn the Spanish into a humming rhythm without understanding, as if it were a religious chant from the Middle Ages. Sometimes a solitary child got on somewhere, going nowhere, and sang a sad, scratchy ballad for donations. Elvis never started so poor.

Meanwhile, at the house, Tom and Angie's sex life seemed engineered to remind me of my monastic chastity. Several times a night I woke to the rhythmic banging of Tom's brass bed against the wall, and Angie's cries were never stifled. They pierced me like poison arrows. I knew she wanted me to feel the pain of her pleasure. One night I dreamed Angie's face was a mask laughing and floating at me through Tom's bedroom wall.

Temporarily, we were brought together when everyone in the house contacted scabies, those dreadful little skin mites my grandfather called the "seven year itch." At the pharmacy we bought a lotion that smelled like gasoline. Every night for two weeks Tom and Angie bathed each other with that vile-smelling tonic. One night I accidentally walked into Tom's room while Angie was rubbing him down. They were both naked. "God damn it, get out of here," Angie screamed, throwing the nearly empty bottle at my head. Carlota screeched and jumped off her perch, chasing me from the room. Embarrassed, I hurled myself down the stairs.

"Damn it John, get lost," Tom yelled behind me.

I turned to the mountains for company. Marty and I climbed the giant Pico de Orzaba, the breast of Ixtla and Popo several more times. Like the drunken diplomat in Lowry's novel, I needed a tonic to survive and the volcanos were that tonic, my present whiskey. Each climb became a creation. I created by connecting myself to these monoliths and their myths and I destroyed that creation on every descent. I wanted to become a castle built upon the dark sands of the volcanoes.

When I wasn't climbing mountains, I took advantage of my imposed freedom by becoming a nomad of the local culture, exploring art museums and my favorite haunt, the Museum of Archeology. I became engrossed with the paintings of Jose Orozco and David Sequeiors. Orozco painted Poncho Villa, but he didn't portray him as a hero. Naked victims, their helplessness exposed to the world, cowered at his feet, and his strength only portrayed their suffering. I couldn't have eaten breakfast below this painting. And Sequeiors disturbed me with his false prophets, but I enjoyed being disturbed. I visited *The Devil in The Church* three times in one weekend, observing the monster savior descending on the faithful multitude, their arms extended in invocation.

My father wouldn't have approved of my cultural taste because Sequeiors was a communist. My father had thrown his cigarette lighter at the Beatles when they appeared on the Ed Sullivan show in 1964. "Communists," he hollered, as if these long-haired boys were going to appropriate his 1954 Ford custom. He thought they could destroy his ordered world, corrupt me and invade the morals of American society, changing them with a few loud strums of their guitars. In a sense he was right, but it was a long time after the spent applause of the sixties before I felt the change. He wouldn't know about my flight and the broken world that preceded it. He wouldn't know about Mexico and the dead beggars whom I had stepped over at the metro stop, their drool unwinding like twisted thread on the broken pavement. And he wouldn't know about the whores, booze and drugs that became my Mexican mantra, my waiting call. What would he know? Before cancer ruined it all, perhaps that kid with the Nellie Fox bat swung over his shoulder, standing proudly in his new Little League uniform and waiting to bat clean-up or sitting in Denny stadium on a cool afternoon, proud to take his son to an Alabama football game with tickets he couldn't afford. I got cokes, too. But that was before Mexico.

In the paintings time stopped, but in the Museum of Antropology it dissolved, its salt dispersing into the murky, liquid future. My favorite artifact was the Sun Stone, the Aztec wheel of time. In its center was the face of an Aztec god Tonatiu clutching his meal of human hearts and on its outside, surrounding the graphics of time's measures, were the tails of serpents touching at the top. Archeologists say that its symbols were once set in turquoise and jade, giving depth and color to death and the Aztec eras of apocalypse. But it wasn't its physical splendor that entranced me, or its collage of symbols. It was its vanished memory. What didn't remain of these people was their memory, that is, the memory of them individually, their postcards to the future. Sure, we had their rocks in glass cases surrounded by security guards, but their essence had already been swiped, vanished with thieves who were still on the run, running with past history into the hideouts of time, and leaving only Indians selling candy on the street, their ribbons, the currency of their past, as useless as Confederate money.

When I wanted company I spent time with McNapp. For a while I didn't want to see Angie, Margarita, Tilly or any other bothersome woman who had arguments, advice, concern or anything I didn't want. I didn't even want to talk with my mother on the phone. I wanted to avoid emotional gymnastics and the only women McNapp liked besides his wife were prostitutes. So one night in February, McNapp asked me to go with him to a few of his favorite Mexico City places, not the places of guidebook warnings, but places where limos ran, not taxis, and tourists weren't on the menu.

First, we ate eat at La Paloma Blanca, an exclusive restaurant in Chapultepec Park. The Maitre'd and waiters knew McNapp by name. "Just some places my friends own," he explained shyly. "I help them out a bit."

McNapp ordered the most expensive items on the menu: Duckling Oruennaise with a 1961 French Burgundy and pastry for dessert. "Ya know, I hate that damn pizza," McNapp admitted. "This is the way real people eat. I come here as often as I can."

"Gets kind of expensive, doesn't it?"

"No mate, it's on the house."

Next, he drove to the rich Las Palmas section of the city. We parallel parked and walked from the sidewalk down a flight of stairs to a narrow metal door. McNapp took a key from his pocket. Inside was the most beautiful whorehouse I had seen in Mexico. It wasn't glitzy here. The women were dressed in silk and moved with the grace of flying swans to the music of a small orchestra, tables were covered with Sevillian tablecloths and drinks were served from platters in crystal glasses. It was obvious that no Saturday night slicks came to this place. There was no Mexican atmosphere. It was more like the pictures I had seen of the Copacabana during the fifties. I half-expected the orchestra to break into *New York, New York*.

"Like it," McNapp asked after we were seated.

"It's different, not your everyday brothel."

"See the man in the white," McNapp nodded toward him. "That's the Mayor of Mexico City. And that man with the red tire is the French ambassador. This is where the big boys go, mate."

"What's the name of this establishment?"

"It doesn't have one."

It was then that I noticed the Colonel. He was wearing tails and had an empty chair at his table. He seemed to be carrying on a conversation.

"And that's the old Colonel, our mutual friend," McNapp said, motioning for him to join us. "He has some connection with the government here. God knows what. He's daffy as hell. They say he only likes his whores if they dress up like Castor. And he orders them special."

"Well boys, I see you found each other," the Colonel said, standing behind McNapp's chair. "I won't be seated, haven't got the time. There's a little lady waiting for my company."

"Aren't you getting a little old for this kind of stuff, hero," McNapp joked.

"Hell no, I remind them of their daddies," The Colonel retorted smiling. "And what was it old Yogi said, 'it ain't over till it's over.'"

"He was talking about baseball, not sex," I playfully reminded him.

"No, young man," he argued seriously. "He was talking about everything. Keep those words in mind."

"Yes sir," I said saluting.

"You know, I get sentimental in this place sometimes." The Colonel rested his eyes on the orchestra. "That's a Benny Goodman tune they're playing," he said. "But I don't remember its name." He moved his finger and pointed it like a pistol at his temple. "This ain't as good as it used to be. I even forget my associates' names sometimes, those that are still around, that is. Business isn't as personal anymore and people move too fast. There isn't any loyalty anymore. That why I like you, McNapp. You understand who your friends are."

McNapp removed a pack of Salem cigarettes from his coat and pounded its bottom on the table to loosen them. "I don't' smoke those Mexican brands," he said to me. "They stink."

"All that's missing here is a casino, somewhere to try your luck on any given day," the Colonel said, tapping his whiskey glass on the table as if he were calling for another blackjack card. "You like gambling?" he asked me.

"Not really, just a little poker every now and then."

"Why don't you play more?"

"I lose too much."

"You must believe its luck."

"I do."

"Well, you're wrong." The Colonel lit his pipe and puffed hard, drawing the fire into the stem. He inhaled the smoke. Then paused, looking like a philosopher expounding on a problem. "It's a matter of character, the other guys. You bet against character. If you can't tell about character, you can't win." Coming from a man whose companion had been a no-character, I thought this insight was unusual. But I didn't comment. I was a little intimdated by the Colonel.

"I'll take my luck in business," McNapp said. "Good hard work, the right investments and timing. To hell with character."

"Ahh, yes. That's why we have you on our team McNapp, to keep us practical. And speaking of practical, call me soon about that other business we discussed last week", the Colonel said, his demeanor becoming stern. "We can't wait too much longer. I'll be through in Haiti soon." He pushed back his chair and put out his pipe, returning it to his pouch.

"I'll call ya next week. I've still got some things to look over," McNapp said.

"I'll be waiting. We'll be counting on you," the Colonel instructed as he walked away. "And oh yes," he said glancing over his shoulder. "Be careful."

"He seems pretty popular for a crazy man," I observed.

"Sometimes they're the smartest ones," McNapp said. "And they can get things done that other people can't. People are always a little afraid of the unpredictable. They always know what you're going to do, but you don't know what they're going to do. They're the ones who have the advantage."

McNapp motioned for a tall mulatto girl. She came, not eagerly, with an air of reserve. Her wrap-around tight white dress hugged her curvy, lithe figure, and her eyes were deep black like narrow caves.

"You want her, we'll take her," McNapp proposed. "It's on me."

"How much," I asked curiously.

"Three-hundred dollars a night for any girl here, no bargaining and nothing by the hour. They don't work for the god damn union." McNapp pulled out a chair and seated her like a lady. Iced champagne arrived immediately, moisture already beading on the metal bucket. "She is something," he patted her hand, sealing the deal. "And look around for some others. I've got some important business people coming into town next week and I'll need some good girls for a party."

"About how many," I inquired.

"About thirty," he estimated. You think that you can last as a talent scout?"

"Damn McNapp, that's nine thousand dollars for whores," I said after a calculating pause.

"Not really, they're on the house, ya know."

We drank Wild Turkey while the girl sat impatiently sipping Brut. I was amazed by this a la carte of beauties and I wanted to take my time. "Thirty women," I mumbled to myself. And I had cried over one before. I wondered what Evelyn would have thought if she could see me now, a connoisseur of women, albeit prostitutes, but no longer shackled to her. I felt my talents were improving. If she ever saw me again, and I wanted to make sure she would, I would be a man of the world, a mountaineer, lover and intellectual, a renaissance man far beyond her Tuscaloosa confines. At the very least, I would be a man who had fucked the whores that other important men had fucked. I would have been in the wombs where power played and I would return with their secrets.

With the next drink, the waiter brought McNapp a note. McNapp's face tensed as he read it, his eyes squinting despite the ample light. "Let's go," he demanded suddenly. "I've got to get out of here."

He waved the girl away. I didn't ask any questions; he was too serious. When we reached the door McNapp pushed me in front of him. "You go first," he commanded. I hesitated. "For your own good, go!" He nudged me in the back, his finger sharp as a knife point.

I walked hurriedly with McNapp shadowing me. His car was squeezed in from the front and back by two Mercedes. After we plunged into his car, he floorboarded the accelerator, smashing first into the front car and then, changing gears, slamming into the other one. "I've got to get out of here," he repeated.

"Who was the note from," I asked as we sped into La Reforma.

"The Colonel." McNapp glanced into his rear-view mirror.

We were nearly to the house before he spoke again. "Hell, this car's only an old Oldsmobile," he said. "I should be driving something else.

14

I got to run to keep from hiding,
And I'm bound to keep on riding,
but I've got one more silver dollar,
But I'm not gonna let them catch me
No I'm not gonna let them catch me
Midnight Rider

—Gregg Allman

The Mexican night went on forever. The last bus followed its yawning path into the mouth of the mountains. Passengers aboard grunted and snored, easing the tensions of fathomless nightmares. Occasionally, lips smacked as someone downed gulps of tequila.

Easter vacation brought a parting of our travel ways. Tom and Angie had left several days before to see the Mayan ruins of the Yucatan. I wasn't invited. I didn't even know they were going until they left. I decided to take the second class Flecha Oro bus to Puerto Esconditio, the beautiful hidden port on Mexico's wild southwestern shore. It was an annual pilgrimage for surfers, European druggies, burned-out Nam vets and flea market entrepreneurs.

Margarita cuddled close to me, almost in my lap she sought warmth from the chill air rushing through the cracked windows. Like a rocking cradle, her breast shifted to a steady rhythm. She dreamed. Her desperate hands gripped my arm and then released tension. I became an unconscious character in the night struggles of her separate world. But which struggle was she dreaming? Was she tearing herself free from a desperate blond prince or committing herself to his embrace? Not that it was important to her. Nothing would change in her real world, at least nothing that I could tell.

"Oye, senor. Tequieres mota?" A fellow rider whispered to me from the seat behind. The strong sweet smell of Mexican marijuana curled into my nostrils. No Mexican night ride is complete without it.

"Si, Gracia." I inhaled deeply and held. My lungs ached. They always did when I smoked pot. I have been a non-smoker since the age of three when I inhaled the cap smoke from a toy pistol and singed my throat.

"Es de Popo," my smoking companion informed me. The fields below the volcano produced the best marijuana in all Mexico. On my climbing expeditions there I saw government troops, the dreaded federales, guarding the small dirt trails leading to the crops in the valley.

I relaxed, sipping the night through my grass straw. Quiet sounds were broken only by the uneven grating of gears as our bus dropped into a valley only to lunge again toward the roofless sky. I knew I was alone. That personal mythology that I wanted to create was deflating like a tire with a slow leak. I was more Mr. Goodyear than Cortez. Margarita stirred. The driver stretched us into a halt. Our bodies fought the motion as the bus slowed before the lights.

We stopped at the Pemex station to change a tire. Despite the late hour, Indian women hawked tortillas and refried beans from their straw baskets. Most were ageless, fat and toothless, the marks of single-diet poverty. I bought a couple of tacos and ate them with hot sauza and tequila. They heated my plumbing, Mexican Draino. "Donde esta el bano," I urgently requested of the Pemex attendant.

I followed the backyard path and I reached a small clapboard shack. At the door sat an usher with owl eyes and a wispy mustache. His greedy hands held a splotched roll of white toilet paper, my ticket. "Uno peso senor," he demanded. For this bribery I received one small square of paper from a roll that must have contained thousands. Well, I figured, every billionaire followed one great precept to success and this tycoon's was "Every man needs a clean asshole."

Margarita was still curled inside her sweater. Carefully, I took my position beside her. I didn't want her to awaken. I wanted to remain alone, a solitary midnight rider. I had brought her along for sex and comedy and truthfully, she was usually a pain in the ass. She was there for image and experience. I wanted to show my world that I was an earthy conquistador, a builder of legends but that notion was fading. I didn't know what she felt and I didn't care. Her feelings were father from me than Pluto. Right now, she was no more than a sperm shot in the hollow dark. After our first few rough confrontations, I had turned sex with her into a fantasy. I loved to observe her, to become a mentally detached third person, to become my own spectator. When I entered her she squirmed and wiggled like a garden snake, her face contorted and her arms and legs began to thrash violently. She became one of those twisted human figures carved in the stone stela the Zapotec Indians called the "Dancers," but in reality they represent deformed individuals who were considered by the Zapotecs to be marked as the gods' favorites.

My arms folded around her and I willed myself into the pastoral could-not-be's. We lived in a grass hut surrounded by flowers. I rested in my hammock, eyes feasting upon a turquoise lagoon with canopies of foliage and purple hills that climbed gently toward distant mountains. Our naked children splashed in the water while fish broiled over hot stones. I drank rum from a coconut shell. Margarita leaned down to kiss me, her dark nipples brushing against my chest. I looked up into the misty morning sky.

It ended with her warm, probing mouth. I came very soon. "Te gusta," she cooed.

"Si, mucho," I answered, still half-dreaming and disappointed. She slept again, squirming restlessly as the bus continued through the mountains.

The dawn was coming as we began our descent from the highest point of the mountains towards Acapulco and the Pacific. "Excuse me. Is Mr. Roosevelt still President of the United States?" a voice asked. Someone in the seat in front turned to face me. My eyes strained to grasp a sold figure from the momentary photographs of passing cars. It was an old woman. Her long braided hair, neatly bound with ribbons, fell over a serape to the seat below. "I speak no English in thirty year. You understand me?" Her voice wheezed like air forced through bellows. Anxiously, she scuffed her huaraches on the metal floor. Several sleepy heads rotated in our direction, probably as surprised as I was that old Mother Mexico spoke English.

"No senora," I replied slowly. "Mr. Ford is now president. There have been many presidents since Mr. Roosevelt. He died a long time ago. Haven't you heard of Mr. Ford?" I peered closely into her face. The wrinkles shaped and defined it like the patters of sand on a windy beach. "Senora, where did you learn English?" I asked.

"I learn it in El Paso. I go to be a singer. I learn English when I wash clothes for North Americano ladies. That is, como se dice, nineteen and thirty-five." The dates gave the woman trouble. Every syllable was a war.

"What songs did you sing," I asked.

"I sing songs of the Mexican cowboys. Canto canciones del campo," she stated proudly.

I could imagine her the heroine of Marty Robbin's *EL PASO*, the beautiful and dangerous Felina of Rosie's Cantina, the girl for whom the cowboy's love was "stronger than death." I could imagine myself shooting that other "wild young cowboy" and then dying in her arms.

"I came home to bring my children back to Mexico, to my family," she said. "See my boys. There, in front." She pointed to three large men chattering into the driver's ear from the seats directly behind the controls. They chuckled as they passed a bottle of tequila to the driver. One man played with the Jesus figure dangling from the rear-view mirror. I imagined that it was one of those bloody crucifixes that looked like a psychopath's victim. Those images were everywhere in Mexico. They had a different Christ, one who didn't play softball for the Northport Baptist church.

"My young son, Pablo, he going to be a movie star. He a cowboy in a movie with Charles Bronson. He make one-hundred dollars. He play a dead man in the street. He have blue eyes. His father is North Americano. You like Mexico?"

"Yes, I live here."

"Why? Why you no live in the United States?" She seemed surprised. "Everybody want to live in the United States."

"I don't know" I covered Margarita's exposed neck with my coat. There was no heat on the bus. "I guess I just have some things to do.

"You like Mexican girls?" she asked, changing the subject again.

"Yes," I lied. "Very much."

"Good, very good." She leaned back into her seat, snuggling her head into a sweater she was using as a pillow.

Dawn's early light opened the sky. We passed a peasant funeral procession on the roadside. Lines of shrouded poor followed a small wooden casket borne aloft on the shoulders of four pallbearers.

Women swayed behind crying in ancient dirges. It was the funeral of a child. A priest carrying a large cross led the solemn crowd. Numberless shacks made of castaway garbage lined the road into Acapulco. A giant sign advertising FIESTA cigarettes covered the whole wall of a hut we passed. We came to the bus station. Hordes of night travelers slept on every available inch of concrete. Naked children laughed as they played in the open sewer nearby. It was the full light of day.

In Acapulco we caught the morning bus to Puerto Escondito. It was a third class bus with machete-toting farmers and a few chickens on board. We passed through the dusty tropical lowlands and ventured into the Guerrero province: guerilla country. Outside the village of San Marcos our bus was stopped by six clean-shaven young men in blue jeans. They carried pistols, but they remained in their holsters while the outlaws went from seat to seat asking for donations. One of them thrust a leather pouch in my face. "Para El Maestro," he said. I nonchalantly dropped in my Timex watch. I needed it less than my money. I was the only Gringo on board and I was afraid of what might happen if I didn't contribute to the cause. I was afraid of what might happen no matter what. Also, I wished his brushfire revolution luck. After all that I had seen in this country, I figured a fellow teacher couldn't do any worse.

The teacher was Lucio Cabanas Barrientos, or "El Maestro," a guerilla folk legend. While serving as a teacher in the rural Guerrero village, he had led a protest demonstration against the expensive school uniforms the poor Mexican children were forced by the government to purchase before they could attend the "free" public schools. The federales fired on this demonstration and several people were killed. El Maestro took to the hills above the town of Atoyac and started an armed resistance against the government. His Party of the Poor roamed the remote Guerrero countryside, attacking government installations at every opportunity. They also bled over onto the highways and stopped buses, asking only for donations from the often sympathetic passengers. It was said they only harmed soldiers and federales. Every couple of months the government controlled newspapers ran stories about his purported death complete with grisly photos of his bloody face. But the people never believed these stories and the guerillas still roved the land.

Margarita was bored with the whole business and a little angry about the unscheduled stop in the heat. She was clearly more interested in showing the guerillas that she had a gringo novillo than in donating to their insurrection. I was surprised they didn't shoot me on the spot for stealing their woman. I was afraid they might see her as a "malinche," a derogatory term referring to the Indian woman who translated for Cortez during the conquest. She became his concubine and the symbol of the treachery of Mexican women toward their men, and also the emblem of foreign domination. Nothing happened. They left with a sincere gracias and a wave of their hands. We were stopped less than five minutes. Quicker than an orgasm the revolution was gone.

For lunch the bus pulled up in Pinotepa Nationale, an all negro town populated by the survivors of slave shipwrecks. I kicked piglets from under our table while I enjoyed cold beer and mole'. The buzz from the marijuana and valium was vanishing. As Tom put it, "the cockroaches were scampering out my ears." I hadn't thought much about Tom and Angie so far. I was making this trip partly to cement my status as odd man out. I wanted it that way. I wanted to create images in solitude and start over yet again, and I didn't think I needed any help.

It was here in Pinotepa Nationale that Margarita broke the news to me that she was a negress. She had tried to tell me before, but with my poor Spanish I translated this confession to mean that she was just dark, or a mestizo. But in this town the ambience clarified the true meaning. It took a physical example. "Mira, Mira, es Margarita," she whispered as she pointed unashamedly at a negro girl who resembled her. She was right. They both had the same features except Margarita was a little lighter. "Oh great, too late now," I thought. But I would've taken her anyway, and enjoyed it even more. I wondered what ole David Bragg would have thought, that is, if he wasn't doing it himself. I laughed to myself. Maybe I should take her home, introduce her to what was left of my family and the boys in my fraternity at the alma mater. Hell, maybe I should marry her.

Before we left, I bought a wedding hammock for us to sleep in when we camped in Puerto Escondito. I was supporting a good cause. These large closely-woven hammocks were made by American prisoners in Mexican jails, and most of them had a while to work on their handicrafts: the automatic seven-year drug sentence with no parole.

The archaic bus backfired out of Pinotepa Nationale and vibrated violently until we reached the Rio Verde river about fifty miles north of Puerto Escondito. Here, we stopped to allow a flatbed truck to cross the narrow bridge from the south. Chained together on the flatbed were five men with long hair, unshaven faces, filthy clothes and bruises that ran together in red and black checkerboard patterns. Dried blood meandered down one's face from a busted eye. His soiled tee shirt read *DALLAS COWBOYS.* "Hippies," Margarita said pointing excitedly. I hoped they were heading for the hammock factory and not a worse fate. The federales in these parts were the most dangerous in all of Mexico. After they had committed crimes in other parts of the country, they were sent to this region to get them out of the way of the tourist and their own people. They were a mean lot.

15

We sputtered into Puerto Escondito at three o'clock Saturday afternoon. It was a one-street town with nick-knack shacks that catered mostly to the international tramp set. There were two new wooden-frame hotels run by enterprising Englishmen, but I chose to hang our hammock in the campground facing the Pacific. It fanned out onto a beach curbed like the inside of a sickle broken by a jetty about one-half mile away. Beyond was a wild cactus-prickly beach known as No Man's Land. The ocean was a surfer's paradise but the ominous riptide claimed several lives a year. A mile or so inland was a federale base.

We ate snapper and lobster broiled in garlic at the campground restaurant. A tall black man in a long-sleeved white shirt and black slacks sat down at the table beside us and unfolded a sheet of black plastic with piano keys printed on its face. His eyes lifted like a preacher's across the campground toward the waves breaking against the jetty. He began to play. A skinny blond with crow's feet crowding her eyes wandered in and sat on the concrete floor. She crossed her legs, placed her chin in her hands and appeared entertained by the silent music. "What are you playing now, Mr. Roberts," she asked when he stopped.

"The 1812 Overture," he replied.

"Oh! One of my favorites," she exclaimed, clapping her bony hands. "Please play louder. Make me see Napoleon's army retreating." Mr. Roberts banged the keys with more enthusiasm.

"He's preparing for his concert," she informed me. Her accent was English. "He's very good you know. He wants to teach the Indian children music. He also paints. As a matter of fact, he painted those fish on the wall." She pointed to a pod of whales swimming over the bartender's head. "The natives call him the smartest man in the world."

"And a school. I want to start a school," Mr. Roberts interrupted while he continued playing. "It will be a good school. People will respect us. It's my gift to Leroy. He didn't have much education."

"Who's Leroy," I asked. He ignored me and kept playing.

"He doesn't talk to anyone but me," said the blond. "Leroy was his friend in the marines. That's his dog tag around Mr. Robert's neck. They lived together here for a while after they got back from the war. He's buried on a small slope just above the jetty."

"I take care of him. Tell them that I take care of him," Mr. Roberts demanded, eyeing his surrogate mouthpiece.

"He takes care of him," she said.

That night Margarita and I were with the camp residents around a beach fire. We passed pot and drank bootleg mezcal, the kind, I was told, containing Spanish fly. Mr. Roberts played his piano while the blonde lady accompanied him on her guitar strumming the Animals' tale of despair:

> *So mother, tell your children,*
> *Not to do what I have done,*
> *Spend your life in sin and misery,*
> *In the House of the Rising Sun.*

After a while I took Margarita and wandered to the other side of the jetty. The moonlight surfed over the swelling waves like a champion on a winning ride and the rip tide was so strong I could see it flowing like a rushing river of light. We stripped and splashed one another in the foam of the roaring surf. Then, we laid our blanket between the soft crevice of two sand dunes. I felt her nipples harden as I pushed into her and her moisture wet my thighs like the bubbles of the surf.

In the silence of the sand I never heard them coming. Suddenly, a spotlight flashed above our naked bodies and federales appeared behind it silhouetted like black ghosts. They were at least a hundred feet away and coming from the jetty's direction. I put my hand over Margarita's mouth and told her to stay down. Our clothes were at the edge of the dunes and I knew they would see them and find us. We had to move quickly. I knew what they would do: take revenge on old Cortez and his Malinche by raping her and torturing and killing me. Almost every week I had heard about tourists disappearing from Mexican beaches. We were the federales' game. They had probably stalked us when we left the campground.

I waited for the light to move beyond us and then led Margarita further behind the sand dunes. I didn't think they would search there because of the Gillette-sharp cactus and sand spurs. This was a luxury outing for them and they wouldn't want to make it difficult. Margarita had the blanket wrapped around her body and her sandals on for protection. I was naked. About a hundred feet behind the dunes, I hid her in a small bowl-shaped depression partially hidden by scrub. I prayed they wouldn't search into this purgatory. In the dawn light, they could spot our trail and pick their way through to us. During the night, I reasoned, they would wait on the jetty where they had a good chance of spotting us if we came close to the beach. They probably wouldn't wait all night to get us, but I couldn't take that chance. I was too afraid I would be wrong.

My mind was working like a computer and I knew I must make instant decisions. I guessed that they thought we would be running together in a panic like a couple of startled rabbits and they would just wait us out, so I picked my way as far behind the jetty as I could go until I hit the barbed wire boundary that marked the federale base. But the scrub was too thick there to continue east toward the campground. I had to make a run toward the beach and hope for the best. I figured they would be shining their light southwest toward the side of the jetty where they had spotted us. An offshore breeze aided me by muffling foot steps and bringing me their talk.

I worked my way out of the scrub about seventy-five feet from the jetty. I lay flat and scouted the men. Just as I thought, they were shining the light southwest away from the campground. They cut off the light. I could see the light from two cigarettes moving slightly. One was breaking the conversation with laughter. They were relaxed. It was high tide and the waves crashed against the jetty and pounded onto the beach with the sound of a building being demolished. I could see their whitecaps marching toward the shore like an invading army on parade. I wanted to time my break to coincide with these soldiers' steps. I didn't want to destroy the rhythm of the sound when I splashed into the water.

I judged I was about fifty feet from the water. I darted straight and low until I slid into the swirling surf. Immediately, I plunged underwater and kicked hard towards the deep. I sensed a wave surge pass over me and I stayed deep enough to feel the sandy bottom hoping I wouldn't be hurled back toward shore. I felt my stomach muscles knot from the held air. Finally, I surfaced. They hadn't seen me. They were facing west and the light was turned off.

I swam parallel to the shore until I reached the campground. I was safe! Saving Margarita was secondary to my own survival but I knew if they caught and harmed or killed her that I would be blamed by the authorities.

The campground concert group had broken up, but Mr. Roberts' blonde companion was still studying the surf with her arms hugging her knees. I crawled to the edge of the surf and called, "Hey, I need help please." I was trying to be calm but my heart was pounding and I couldn't get my breath.

"What's wrong?" she asked sleepily, her mind drug-cloudy. "Why are you naked?"

"Could you get me some clothes?" I asked, suddenly as self-conscious as Adam after the fall.

Slowly, she fetched me an old pair of cut-off blue jeans from someone's clothesline, not bothering to avert her eyes while I stood to put them on. "What happened to you?" she asked, staring at my groin. On the fleshy part of my upper thighs and lower abdomen there were tears like ribbons. I had shredded myself on either the cactus or the barbed-wire, although I didn't remember it.

I ignored the wounds and slipped into the shorts.

"Margarita's hiding on the other side of the jetty and she needs help," I revealed. "The federales jumped us."

Quickly, we assembled three surfers, a Dutch tourist and Mr. Roberts. The Magnificent Seven rode again. Everyone was unarmed except for pocket knives and sticks. No one mentioned the possible consequences as we ran towards the jetty, our own Picketts' charge. The federales turned to face us with their spotlight. I waved my arms over my head and shrieked my best rebel yell. Instantly, they turned the light off and retreated toward No Man's Land. I don't think they feared our shaggy band as much as they feared they might get into trouble for harming so many tourists, and they weren't up for any assignments in an even more remote place.

We found Margarita where I left her. She was a terrorized animal helpless with anticipation. She crept out from her lair, dressed in her discarded clothes and we returned to the campground. She refused to sleep with me in the hammock. Her novel hadn't ended the way she dreamed it would. There was no blonde hero on the front cover, only a bloody gringo, dressed in ill-fitting shorts who wanted to screw her in a remote, dirty campground. Disneyland was never further away.

I gave her money for a hotel room and said good-night.

16

Next morning, Good Friday, a young doctor at the govern ment clinic cleaned my wounds and gave me a tetanus shot. He didn't have any pain pills. These small places rarely had enough needles and bandages, much less medical luxuries. I was lucky they had the tetanus serum. In addition to the rips, my feet were filled with broken-off cactus needles. I was told there was nothing I could do about this except wait for them to work their way out and hope they didn't become infected.

All day I swayed in my hammock and drank Bacardi Rum to relieve my pain. The experience of the previous night had silenced Margarita. She avoided me and spent most of her time talking to the local Mexicans in the campground restaurant. That didn't bother me too much. I read Graham Green's *The Power and the Glory* and learned from a Mexican radio sports broadcast that back in the States Hark Aaron had hit another record home run. But his real quest had ended on April 8 of last year when he had hit number 715 and destroyed a myth by building a new one. The chase was over. At night, my pain subsided and I slept while the cool night breeze rocked me gently.

The next day I left Margarita and boarded the morning bus for Oaxaca. It was a third-class bus with crates of goods bound for the market stacked on top. When the bus circled the mountainous Highway 131, I could feel its weight lean toward the cliffs like a ship listing in a storm. I knew I was moving towards Tom and Angie but I didn't care. I could avoid them.

We were boarded by the federales outside Sola de Vega. They were probably looking for weapons destined for the guerillas, but since I was a gringo, they took a special interest in me. They checked my papers, emptied my pack and asked my why I was going to Oaxaca. Only their whim kept me from joining some other hippies in the back of a truck. You didn't have to commit a wrong to suffer in this country. It was indiscriminate, part of its unnatural order.

By the time we reached Oaxaca in the late afternoon, my feet had begun to hurt badly and I had a fever. I rented a room at the Hotel Central, took some aspirin and soaked my feet in hot water. I wanted to see the sunset at Monte Alban, so I limped downtown and took the tour bus to the mountaintop. The sun was just setting and the sky was streaked with pastels. I sat down on the steps of an ancient ball court and imagined the past games where the winners, not the losers, were sacrificed to the cruel, demanding gods. That gave me a good feeling. At least they couldn't sacrifice me, the loser ultimo. I wanted to explore more but my feet were throbbing and the fever had returned. I felt tired and sleep began to creep over me. I couldn't move and I had no desire to. Here I was in the place where man had invented time and I was slipping out of it. So what. I could die here for all I cared, right here on top of this sacred mountain. I had been on one before.

"John, wake up. Are you OK? Wake up!" Tom was shaking me by the shoulders.

"He's sick," I heard Angie say.

"My feet. It's my feet." I muttered.

"He's got a fever and he's been hurt somehow," Tom said. "What happened to you?"

They helped me to the van, my arms slung over their shoulders, feet dragging behind. "It's a long story," I answered. "It seems like I always have long stories." I was delirious from the fever and kept losing focus. Tom drove me by a closed Seguro Social clinic and then stopped to ask directions to the hospital. "No," I pleaded. "They'll want to know what happened and probably arrest me. Don't. I won't go."

"I think we can take care of this," Angie volunteered quickly. "You're good with your hands. Let's get him back to the hotel."

In their room, one floor above mine at the Hotel Central, Angie boiled water on a camp stove while Tom prepared his first aid kit. "Here, drink this," he ordered, handing me a bottle of Tequila Sauza. "This is going to hurt. Just think of yourself as a piece of sculpture in the making."

I smoked a joint and drank until I could see the lights from the Zocalo moving in waves outside the window. Then Tom began to remove the cactus needles by cutting skillfully around each black dot and then removing as much of it as he could with the tweezers. He boiled out the infection with peroxide. The dope and tequila lessened the pain. "I'm fucking John Wayne," I yelled, imagining a bullet being removed by Doc in the wild wild west, the hero, me, drunk and stoic.

I remember waking in the dead of the night, tossing and sweating. Sleeping again, I dreamed of ancient Mexico. I was with the Zapoteca priest on Monte Alban. They were watching the heavens while they worked on a sacred calendar stone. I was trying to explain to them what I knew about time but they couldn't hear me. My mouth moved without sound. I could feel my frustration trying to force its way out of my guts.

In the morning I awoke weak but cool. The fever had broken and Angie had cleaned my barber-pole wounds again and applied a sulfur cream to the gashes. "Bro, what the hell happened to you? You look like you fought the Aztecs singlehandedly." Tom poured me a fresh glass of cool water from his canteen.

"I did. And I lost," I said.

Bro, you're just lucky we decided to check out Monte Alban again before we left. You're in pretty bad shape."

"You'll be OK for a while," Angie stepped back into the room from the shower, piling her long hair inside a white hotel towel and studying herself in the mirror. "But you need to get treated at the American hospital back in Mexico City. Those wounds could still get infected. Say, don't I sound like a nurse?" She turned quickly revealing her flat waist from the folds of her robe. "Why I'll bet I'm as good as Tilly."

"I hope I don't give you any more practice on this trip." I substituted the water for a shot of tequila, the last of the bottle.

"Where's the worm," Angie took the bottle from me and shook it, looking into it from underneath as if she were studying the stars.

"That's not tequila, it's mezcal."

"Too bad, I've heard that you hallucinate when you eat the worm." She tossed the bottle into the trash. "We're going back this afternoon after we've seen the ruins at Mitla. Maybe I'll find us some mushrooms. Those will help your pain."

"I wouldn't look for any," I warned. I told them about the federale attack, the hippies and the dope check. "There's dangers out there. And there's no protection here."

"But John, as usual, you're sticking you neck out," Angie scolded. "I've talked to people who had no trouble getting mushrooms here. It's all in the way you approach it."

"They're for religious festivals," I retorted. "And people get hot when you mess around with their religion."

"Well, who's to say that I'm not religious," Angie argued. "Anyway, it's all a matter of perceptions."

By high noon we arrived at Mitala. It was Easter Sunday but the only stone that was rolled away was the doorstop used at the door of the small whitewashed church. This church was built over the site of the legendary entrance to the ancient Mixtec underworld, their heaven, hades and hell. This place was corporeal, a place where they left the world to become lost forever in the maze of their own souls. Tom knew the story.

"It was here," he lectured on the steps while Angie took a hit on a joint, "that the Indians came to die. They walked into this church when it was a temple, and entered the caves that led to where no one knows, deep within the earth. They took their worldly riches with them, as many as the could carry, and disappeared, never to return, voluntary suicides, like lemmings walking into the ocean for their baptism of death."

"And the Spanish had the caves sealed," I added. "Despite the riches down there, the place has never been excavated."

"Why," Angie asked.

"Fear of the dead," I answered assuredly.

"Or fear of the living," Tom guessed. "Maybe they were afraid of what they would find and what it might do to them."

Despite the cool valley air, the sun beat down with hammer heat. A dusty haze clouded the sky, the result of the dry season in this forsaken place. Two dark children approached us with hot Coca-Colas to sell.

"Como se dice in Zapoteca," Angie asked, pointing to the name on the bottles.

"Coca-Cola," was the immediate reply.

"Of course," I laughed. "There weren't any Coca-Colas back then. The words are the same as now."

"But the concepts haven't changed," Angie argued. "They must have a word for sweets or good."

"I don't think so," Tom reasoned. "But I'll bet they have a word for those caves."

"Like what?" Angie asked.

"Like Muerta," I answered. "Muerta, Muerta," I shouted at the children, pointing towards the church door. They backed slowly away, hissing to each other in their lost Indian tongue and taking their Coca-Colas with them.

On the road back to Mexico City we had a party. When the van's odometer turned for 49,999 to 50,000 miles, we stopped in the middle of no place on Highway 190 to toast the event with cold Bohemias. Tom set his camera on a tripod and took a photo of us in front of the van. Tom and Angie are relaxed and smiling, Angie curled up against Tom as they leaned back on the bumper, but I have an anguished expression and I'm standing off to the side. The fever was returning.

For three weeks after we returned to Mexico City I was unable to return to school. The doctors at the American Hospital diagnosed me as suffering from para-typhoid, a kidney problem, amoebas, and bacterial infections in my feet and other wounds. Tilly, my loyal Irish nun, took time away from her bullfighter to nurse me. She spoon-fed me papaya and water and slept by my side to sooth my fevered nightmares. I screamed at open doors, dark chases and sudden falls. She anticipated my endings and hushed me with the touch of her hands and the press of her body. I moved against her, feeling myself melting into her and her softness saying "SSShhh. SSShhh, everything will be alright. I'm here. Go to sleep."

Sometimes I made love to her, or maybe it was just a dream.

17

In late April when I returned to school my teaching style had changed. I was no longer interested in the inquiry method, this process of plunging to the depths of things like a salvage diver looking for treasure. Truthfully, I wasn't certain about what the students were supposed to find when they reached this ship of knowledge. I knew whatever it was, I was still searching and wasn't competent to toss them a lifeline. For me, history was losing its focus and becoming less personal. It was zeroing in on me like a telescopic lens, drawing my image closer but leaving my essence in the distance. It didn't care about me and I demanded care.

My teaching became confused. In American history we had reached the Civil War, my specialty. Yet all I concentrated on was the battles, especially the bloody ones like Shiloh and Antietam, futile battles with senseless charges, carnage and no clear victors, battles decided more by chance than bravery. I raved rhetorical questions at my students, questions I knew they couldn't answer because they weren't in their books. "Why," I ranted, "did these men on both sides leave their farms and their women to fight?"

"To abolish slavery?"

"Wrong!"

"To defend their homes?"

"Wrong!"

"Tariffs?"

"Wrong!"

Sweat dripped down my face like hot sauza from a taco. I pushed my hands down on my desk and arched up on my toes, my head extending out over the floor.

"They were bored, damn it. They were bored!"

"Boards? What's board's?" asked one student who wasn't proficient in English.

"Bored," you little idiot. "They hated their smelly farms, unfaithful wives and stupid kids. They hated the snow, rain or heat. They hated themselves and they wanted to become more than they were and the war was their only chance, death be damned. And they didn't give a crap about causes! And you know what most of them died of?" The class sat stunned, afraid to answer. "Diarrhea. They shit themselves to death."

Tilly and I went to the Little Man's store for lunch. Sweat still beaded on my face and my blue shirt was soaked, changing its color to a darker navy. "John, you're still sick," she said, placing her hand over mine. "I heard you yelling across the hall."

"No, it's the arsenic I'm taking for the amoebas. It causes me to sweat a lot." I wiped my face with several of the coarse napkins the Little Man provided.

"That's good. It's like taking a shower from within. It cleans you out. Anyway, I know something that will make you feel better." She looked directly into my eyes, one of her traits that bothered me sometimes. You know Lupita Solice, the school guidance counselor?" Tilly waited for me to nod my affirmation. "She wants to go out with you, despite your bad reputation."

"I don't know Tilly." I wadded up my used napkins and tossed them at a trash box, missing by a few inches. "Mexican girls don't seem to be my type."

"My God, John, I hope you don't judge Lupita by that prostitute Margarita. Lupita is a psychologist who studied at UCLA, and she's a friend of mine. And she comes from a prominent family. Her uncle is the president of PRI."

"Well, she is a looker. And you know I like dark women. I'll give her a try."

"No, I think she'll give you a try." Tilly frowned playfully. "Hurt your reputation. Be a gentleman."

"I'll try," I promised half-heartedly.

Tilly, Lupita and I met at Happy's Pizza that Friday. Quickly, I discovered I enjoyed Lupita's company more than Margarita's. This girl was more than a toy. She was intelligent, well-read and charming. "Do you like Mexican authors?" she asked me after McNapp brought us our first pitcher of beer.

"I don't know. I haven't read any. I've only read about Mexico."

"You should read Octavio Paz and Carlos Fuentas. They will tell you about what Mexico is?" She adjusted her rings, turning them so their setting wouldn't hit the beer glass.

"The students tell me you're more Mexican than they are. Is that so?"

"Probably not." I was secretly flattered. It felt good to have others confirming me. Lupita was already moving into my fortified territory through an open gate. I hoped she was only guessing. I didn't want to share very much. That was one thing I liked about Margarita. She could never really tell anything about me, except that I liked to screw her. And she didn't seem to care.

McNapp had a seafood pizza sent to us, but he declined our dinner invitation. "I'm too busy tonight, mate. I've got to watch the help. It's Friday, ya know?"

But it wasn't that. For some reason McNapp felt uneasy around Tilly and she didn't appear to care for his company either. He seemed to scratch his arms like he was breaking out in hives every time she was around, and she became silent, letting others carry the conversation. "I never liked nuns," he once told me. Ya know, Catholic school and all that."

"Lupita's mother is an archeologist," Tilly said, encouraging my obvious interest in her friend.

"Yes, she teaches at the University of Mexico. Are you interested in archaeology?"

"Yes, very much."

"Then would you like to join me this Sunday for a trip to Teotihuacan? With my mother's permission they will let us go under the temples to see the sites being excavated." She read my eyes and flat, disappointed face. "Don't worry. It'll be just us. Mother will make the arrangements ahead of time."

"Thanks Tilly," I whispered in her ear as we parted. I had expected the Mexican girl next door, complete with crucifix and chaperons. I was happy to be wrong.

The temples of Teotihuacan had been lonely for nearly two thousand years. Lifeless, they had been abandoned by an unknown people who left the scraps of their legacy carved on the stones of other dead cities, the borrowers of their fate.

Lupita and I were under the Temple of the Moon in a restricted area. Guard rails separated us from the colorful paintings on these subterranean walls. The color was the difference. Above ground, the murals and carvings had been bleached and mutilated by the sun, wind and rain, but here they were protected in the dark, cool deep freeze of their own solitary and strange heaven.

"What happened to these people here? Why did they leave?" I asked, while gazing at the dark red image of a feathered serpent, cracked and expanded by time.

"No one knows for sure." Lupita brushed the dust from her jeans. "Some archeologists say drought or famine. Others say religious fanaticism based on the predictions of their priest.

Supposedly, they left because they were told it was the end of their world. But nobody knows. They were only a legend when Cortez came."

"Well, they were right. Their world ended. Can't the world be a state of mind?"

"Yes, Mr. Plato, but that state of mind can mirror reality." She pointed at the feathered serpent on the wall. "That's Quetzalcoatl." I peered across the rail. The painting looked like a lazy medieval dragon, smiling, sleeping on its paws and waiting for Beowulf. "His legend says that he grew sick of human sacrifice and left this land, only to return someday to redeem his true followers and claim his rightful throne. Sound familiar? And Montezuma thought Cortez was Quetzalcoatl, so he feared him and welcomed him into Tenochtitian. And it was the end of their world and all the peoples before them, the end of time."

Despite the "No Tocar" sign I reached across the barrier and touched the image. I was hoping to feel the electricity of life in something so long dead. But it was cool and smooth, as if its life, or predicted death, had faded into the stone walls. There was nothing left but our perceptions. "I don't think he's coming back anytime soon," I said.

We also climbed the pyramids of the sun and the moon. It was noon and the sun beat down on their apexes with the ferocity of a war drum. "This land was once fertile." Like an ancient empress surveying her domain, Lupita spread her arms over the valley. There was nothing green and no sign of water, not even an oasis. The land was as yellow and dry as a potato chip. I thought I smelled salt in the air, and my skin was powered with a white film.

"Now I know how the mummies feel." I scratched my arms. "But I think I prefer a pickle jar."

"Do you believe there's magic in pyramids?" Lupita asked, fixing her eyes on a village to the east.

"The conditions in this place would argue no, unless the gods want it that way."

"Maybe it's just waiting, being saved for a resurrection. Who knows, this may be the future." Lupita kneeled and scratched the surface of the pyramid with one of her long, red fingernails.

"Nothing under there, just rock," I said.

"It will take a long time, the change." Slowly, she drew a small circle and placed a dot in its center. "That's us, we're it. It's our responsibility."

"Since when," I chuckled.

Lupita placed her arm through mine. "Would you like to meet my uncle, the politico? He likes North Americans. He went to Harvard."

"Sure, even though I hate Harvard men." Lupita bristled for an instant, not understanding my jovial prejudice.

"Oh, no you don't." She tapped me on the shoulder with her fist. "We'll go for dinner. I'll call him."

We ate lunch close to Teotihuacan in a restaurant located in an underground cavern. It was the only good place to eat between that dead city and the outskirts of Mexico City. It was also the only cool place. Water from a subterranean stream cascaded in narrow rivulets down its rock walls and was circulated by an aqueduct that rounded the dining area. We drank cool white German wine and enjoyed Spanish chicken with black olives.

"So this is where the water went," I said, touching the moisture on my wine glass with my fingertip. "Maybe after the resurrection you spoke of, this is where the people will live."

"Yes. An escape from a parched world. Here in Mexico, water is life. This could be a future Noah's ark."

"Or a fallout shelter."

"A fallout shelter? What is a fallout shelter?"

"During the early sixties Americans were afraid of the Atomic bomb. Some people bought or built underground shelters to live in in case of attack. They had air purifiers and storage space for canned foods and such. My father and I used to look at the different models at the county fair. I remember that the air purifiers worked by turning a hand crank that drew the air in from outside and through a charcoal filter. Even then, I couldn't see how that would work. How many years could a family keep going before their arms fell off from exhaustion." I meant to be funny, but Lupita didn't laugh.

"Wanting life could keep them going."

"Or the fear of death. Isn't it the same thing?"

"No, life is hope."

"Did you learn that at UCLA?"

"No, in Mexico."

I was beginning to enjoy this attractive, cultured woman, so different from the rough peasant Margarita. I hoped those days were over.

Before we left to visit Lupita's uncle, we returned to my place for refreshment. After another bottle of white wine we kissed and listened to the Beatles' *Abby Road* album. Lupita hummed the rhythm while I moved my kisses over her neck and breast. Her eyes closed and she rested her head against my back. "Would you like to make love," she asked.

I led her upstairs to my room, and Lupita removed my conquistador mask. She set it face down on top of my bookcase. "I don't like that thing looking at us," she said, removing the rest of her clothes and laying down, waiting for me.

Unlike Margarita, she was petite and the color of a new penny, her bedroom manners were gentler and during sex her smell was not musky but more like old clothes taken out of a wooden trunk after being hidden for many years. I liked it. We continue making love until late afternoon.

Munoz Leydo was tall, Spanish-white and dressed informally in beige slacks and a blue polo shirt. He extended his hand immediately and shook mine softly without the macho squeeze I had come to expect from affluent Mexicans. "I'm so glad to meet you," he said, breaking the handshake. His accent was more Oxford than Harvard. "Teachers are always welcome here, especially North American ones." He placed his hands on my back and gently guided me around the edge of his tiled swimming pool and into his study. "Let's enjoy a drink while the ladies prepare for dinner. I'm a little old fashioned. I believe men need some time together. Socialize."

Classical music poured from built-in speakers on each wall. "Please sit down," he said, pulling out a leather-cushioned chair for me. It had a high back and its wood was carved with designs. "It's from Castille, fifteenth century. I like to sit in one of these when I work." He sat across from me in an identical chair. There were six in the room. He sat regarding me for about a minute without speaking and then he asked, "Do you like the music, it's Wagner."

"Yes, it's nice."

"No, no" He locked his fingers together and placed his hands on his lap. "Actually its somewhat harsh." He smiled to show this disagreement wasn't a rebuke. "I like it because it helps me to think practically, correctly. You see, I admire the Germans more than any other peoples in the world. You'll notice many of my books are by them. Something to drink?" He broke off and went to his liquor cabinet. Quickly, I surveyed the titles of his books, squinting to cover the distance. Many were histories of the Third Reich, including Hitler's *Mein Kempf* and most were written in German. "Bourbon or Scotch?" He returned with a bottle of each and two glasses. An Indian servant dressed in a white coat magically appeared with a bowl of crushed ice.

"I'll take the Black Jack," I answered. "On the rocks." The young man in the coat poured me a full glass. Munoz Leydo took his Johnny Walker straight, without ice. Quietly closing the door, the servant left the room.

"Lupe tells me you teach history," he said after sipping his scotch. He seemed to be a man of pauses, waiting for responses like a teacher who enjoys making students squirm when he knows they don't know the answer to his questions. I was uncomfortable, feeling I had made a mistake, a wrong answer, before I made it.

"Yes, for now. But I really think I had rather teach literature."
I felt the "r's" roll off with a little of his accent.

"Oh, that's too bad." His eyebrows dropped in genuine disappointment. "I don't' get as much out of literature as I do history, especially German history. You see to me history is about cause and effect, and literature is about confusion. That's why I admire you North Americans almost as much as the Germans. If you could only turn your history into culture the way Germans do, ahh yes. Do you like Mexico?" Again he suddenly shifted subjects, as if his concentration had blown a fuse. He reached over and topped my glass off, even though I had only drunk a sip.

"Yes. And I think it's the confusion I like."

"Of course. But what you North Americans like is not confusion but change. You must remember that here in Mexico because we never really change." I was a little angry because I didn't like anyone telling me how I felt. But knowing that he meant no harm, I masked my feeling. This was his country and I was his visitor. My students may have thought I was more Mexican than most Mexicans, but I was learning that I wasn't.

After a meal of steak and lobster my host toasted "North American success and practicality" with Napoleon Cognac. It flowed into my stomach like lava, dissolving the residue of the pyramids.

"My uncle likes you," Lupita observed as she drove her imported Volkswagen back through her uncle's guarded gates. "He told me that if you ever need his help, just call him."

"Why would I need his help?" I rolled up the window to shield the dusty, polluted wind.

"John, this is Mexico," she said.

18

In May, Angie returned to Minnesota for a short visit with her father. She had accepted an English teaching position at the American School for the next year and she continue to live with us. She and Tom were to continue as lovers. No other plans were apparent beyond this treaty and I didn't expect any.

I suspected that Tom, with his magnetic attraction to Angie, would sink into one of his maniacal depressions where he ranted and raved about every little thing, or stayed in his bed as if he was timing a creeping cancer of the gut. I was wrong. He began to thumb through his *PEOPLES GUIDE TO MEXICO* in search of a place to go. Vacation was coming up and he seemed to regain that sense of individual freedom that drove him on the road. I pulled out the old AAA road map and we plotted our points. The May vacation was a lengthy two-week break provided by the Mexican government as a response to the religious Semanta Santa holidays sponsored by the Catholic church. The officially atheist Mexican rulers had to be one-up on the Pope and show the citizens just who really was boss. We decided on a barnstorming ride through Southern Mexico, Guatemala and Belize. Tom wanted to add Belize when he read that "most tourists want to avoid Belize because of its backward transportation system and total lack of resorts. "That's the place for us," he stated enthusiastically. "We want to go where nobody else wants to go. It's bound to be a wonderful place, Bro."

I was surprised that I was also excited about another trip to backward places, but once again I let Tom's daring get under my skin. My fears had healed along with my ripped legs and punctured feet. There would be no women on this trip and I felt that would alleviate most of the danger. They seemed to drag my mortality around with them and step on it every now and then. Also, I felt that old sense of brotherhood with Tom returning, the feelings that I had before Angie and the rest.

Before we left, we were required to get another smallpox vaccination and shots for typhoid and malaria. The clinic that gave these was located across the street from the Soviet embassy. While standing in line waiting my turn, I couldn't help but contemplate that massive grey compound. What went on over there and who knew about it? It was an intimidating place that looked like Dracula's blood bank and it made me value my freedom even more. I felt that someone over there was watching me, but for what I didn't know. I felt that some morning I might be summoned, or to some other place like it, for my own Kafkaesque trial.

We were protected against disease but not against the federales, border guards, village police and other protectors of the people. It was a long ride to Belize, most of it through the crooked finger of Mexico and all the dangers of the wilds. We would be traveling in Tom's Van. We had long hair, embroidered shirts and we were gringos, so to the uniformed authorities, we were hippies. But, Lupita and Munzo Leydo came to our rescue. She had Senor Leydo draw up a document that declared Tom and me "special guests of the Mexican government" and it was signed by Senor Leydo himself. It was our own Declaration of Independence from hassle.

On the morning of May 17, we left for the legendary Isthmus of Tuhuantepec and the town of Juchitan, noted mostly for its beautiful women. I had read from my history and anthropology books that these lovely ladies were a mixture of the native Polynesian stock who paddled and blew over from the Pacific Islands and the French railroad workers who tried to lay tracks through here in the previous century. This made the same mixture as Tahiti.

We took the familiar Oaxaca highway and stopped in its namesake, the city of my rescue. We decided to spend the night in a campground and to skip any sightseeing. We had seen most of it before. Besides us, an old tanned sea-dog of a fellow parked his Dodge van, painted lavishly with red, purple and green flowers. Fishing equipment littered the back. He ambled over good-naturedly to make conversation and share stories. "Where ya heading boys," he asked with an accent that sounded like the Maine shore.

"Eventually Belize," Tom answered. "Anything you can tell us about it?"

"If you're going there, you already know enough. I just hope you have some heavy-duty shocks on that Chevy."

"Roads that bad, huh? Tom asked.

"Well, I'll put it this way," he answered, puffing on his pipe and talking simultaneously. "Are you two friends?" We nodded. "Well you won't be when you get off those roads in Belize." He laughed and puffed, the smoke trailing away in the mild breeze.

By noon the next day we were driving down the dusty streets of Tehuantepec. "It says here this place is a matriarchy," I summarized from one of my books. "In other words, the women are in charge."

"Hell, John," he laughed. "You don't need a book to tell you that."

I looked up from my reading and saw Amazons weighing at least three-hundred pounds proudly strutting towards the market. Behind them, wiry men in Mexican whites struggled with the heavy boxes of merchandise. One group of women with balloons in their hair passed by the window. "Donde esta senorita," Tom called to one.

"Una marcha nupcial," she answered.

The women were dressed in patterned silk dresses and the balloons stuck out of their heads like comical horns. These rubber condiments of the new world were on their way to a wedding march. I wondered if they threw these balloons on the bride and groom rather than rice.

We stopped at the market where Tom bought a silk dress for Angie and added another mask to his collection, the face of a cat-like animal, perhaps a jaguar, and possibly a god from a forgotten pantheon. I had begun to understand Tom's obsession with masks. He had become a librarian of dead and dying rituals, a receptacle of the past scrap pages, even though it wasn't his past.

We continued to the beach at Salina Cruz for lunch and a siesta. There wasn't much there except two little thatched-roofed restaurants and the wildest beach I'd ever seen. We were there at high tide and the crashing waves roared like canons. Rocks protruded from the sands like castles in Spain from the hilltops and I heard their call when the waves' power died in their crevices.

After a lunch of broiled fish and beer, I took a walk about a mile down the beach, avoiding the urge to swim because of shark fins cutting through the surf like silent speedboats. I stopped before I lost sight of the restaurant hut, afraid of an Easter repeat I needed to mend, not be torn apart again. Slowly, fear was beginning to creep into my gut like a noisy burglar. I wasn't sure I was getting what I needed out of Mexico. I had left the States to escape my own abyss, but I had plunged into something even darker, a watery cave that had only led me, gasping for air, into the ocean of the lost.

When I returned, Tom was swinging an Amazon in a hammock by the hut. She was larger than any of the ones I had seen in Tehuantepec. She was fanning herself and held out the fan to me to continue the chore. She was conversing in broken Spanish and asking Tom about life in the Estados Unitos. Every minute or so she could roll her eyes at him and say, "Muy Bonito." Tom had on his *A WOMAN'S PLACE IS ON TOP* tee-shirt and I envisioned Tom smothered beneath this elephant of sex.

On the other side of the hammock was a young girl who looked like an actress in a visit Hawaii commercial: dark moist skin, glistening black eyes, long silky black hair, ripe breast and the face of an angel. She was staring at Tom who was making lizard faces at her. He turned up his nose with his fingers and stuck out his tongue between the spaces in his crooked teeth. She giggled innocently.

"You want to marry my daughter?" the Amazon casually asked Tom. She didn't even open her eyes. "We can go to Tehuantepec today." She yawned. "I always wanted her to marry someone from Los Estados Unitos. Do you want her?"

A young man in jeans was standing in the door of the restaurant watching us intently. He obviously had some stake in this girl. But he didn't move and his face was passive. I thought maybe he had been promised this girl before Tom showed up with his reptilian charm.

Tom dropped his hand from his nose and his tongue disappeared inside his mouth. "Yes," he replied without hesitation.

"Bueno," the Amazon shouted as she reached for Tom to lift her from the hammock. "Follow us into Theuantepec and the wedding will be tonight!" She waved for the young man in the door and she piled into an old fifties Buick with him and the nymph. She waved for us to follow and circled towards the road to town.

"Shit, Tom, what the hell are you doing?" I asked as we trailed the Buick. "These people may be serious and then you will be stuck in this Mexican coffin for a long time. How do you think you'll get out of here once you marry her."

"Oh, calm down Bro," he said. "It wouldn't be so bad would it. Isn't that what you wanted, too? Sit back with a pretty little girl in a hammock swaying in the breeze. Not a care in the world. Some men would give millions of dollars for this and it's all mine free for just a little time."

"You're not serious."

"Hell no," he replied. "This is just for one night. You spend the night in the van and tomorrow I'll go out for a cup of coffee, you pick me up, and off we go to Belize. I'll get at least one night."

"God, Tom, it may not be that easy," I pleaded. " We don't know these peoples' customs. It may be a long time before you get out of here, if you get out of here. I know one thing. I'm not risking my neck. If you marry that girl, I'm leaving on the bus. Adios!"

"Just one night," Tom begged. "Just let me have that baby for one night. I can see it now, a clean little hairless pussy with just a red dot in the middle. I want one, just one, before she gets all fouled up."

The Buick speeded up and we almost lost it at an intersection of gravel roads. "He's trying to lose us," Tom said.

"No shit," I responded. "And I'll bet you know why."

When we reached Highway 190, Tom slowed down and the Buck vanished from sight. He pulled into a Pemex station, turned around, and we headed toward the beautiful women of Juchitan.

"I could've used one night, John. Just one night," he said.

We rolled into Juchitan that evening and quickly noted the deserted streets, closed stores and roadblocks in the zocalo. All the life was coming from the south end of town where a faint glow hovered over the horizon like an umbrella. We had found the fiesta. Juchitan's yearly fiesta began on May 19 when the whole town, following patterns that we can no longer fathom, gathered to celebrate some aspect of life's renewal. This was a place where myth was alive.

We parked the van in the empty zocalo and walked to the festivities. A large tent covered a one-block area and around the tent numerous goodies, foods and drinks were being sold. Before we had a chance to buy a beer, a slightly borracho young fellow appeared and placed a couple of Carta Blancas in our hands while he led us inside the tent, crammed with colorful ladies dressed in silks. Their hair was braided down to their waist in decorative ribbons, there were no balloons here, and some of them wore the tall beautiful headdresses that flowed down the profiles of their faces. The men all wore clean pressed whites and new straw hats. Most were dancing, even the children.

We sat down in two of the metal chairs surrounding the dance area and enjoyed our beers. Many of the dancers turned and smiled at us and danced closer to our seats. They seemed to be dancing for our pleasure. "Hey, Tom," I observed. "I think we may be the honored guest."

"Yeah, and look around," he said. "We're the only tourists here. Maybe we're the attraction."

After two long tunes, the music stopped. The couples, young and old, congregated and then lined up before our chairs.

"What's this?" Tom asked. "You've done the reading."

"I don't know," I answered. Maybe they're going to ask us to dance."

"I can't dance. I look like the scarecrow in The Wizard of Oz, flopping all over the place."

"Then just move around. It's probably only a courtesy."

The first couple stepped forward with the man's hand lightly holding the lady's arm. They were a middle-aged couple, but the woman still had that smooth, dark beauty of this area. "Do you wish to spend the night with my wife tonight?" her husband asked us both in Spanish.

I didn't wait for Tom to respond. I was afraid of what his answer might be. Thinking quickly, I knew this couldn't be real. Obviously, every man in the line was going to ask us the same question. The challenge was how to avoid insulting them.

"No Gracious," I responded. "But I am honored. Your wife is very beautiful and this is a lovely fiesta." The man appeared satisfied and spun off to his right with his bride as if he were spinning out of an Alabama square dance while the next couple repeated the invitation. Tom caught on and soon began to parrot my reply. As their guests, we were entitled to the ultimate courtesy, but it was only a gesture. In return, they expected an acknowledgement of this honor. But I couldn't help but wonder, as I'm sure Tom did, just what would have happened if we had said "yes!"

After the last couple, a drunk and soiled old man with a drooping mustache much like Tom's appeared out of the night and staggered towards us. "Gringos, Chinga su Madres," he yelled, waving his empty tequila bottle at us. For a few seconds I was afraid, as if this whole fiesta was merely a plot to capture gringos and destroy them. But my fears were unfounded. Several other men led the shouting soldier away and the dancing began again.

Tom and I began to shoot Mescal with our beers. Soon we were drunk. Two teen girls dressed in their finery asked us to dance and before long we were swinging circles, giving at least some pretense of dancing. We danced for a while and then weaved our way with the girls' help to the van. The one who chose me couldn't have been more than fourteen, but the one with Tom was older and had a tall, stately grace. She climbed into Tom's van with him and soon I heard the soft creaking of the shocks. Meanwhile, I stayed outside with my little girl and drank a beer while she asked me about life in the United States. We spoke in English, the best English I heard in Mexico.

The next morning I lifted my concrete eyes and discovered I had slept on the sidewalk. Tom was twisting and rumbling along in the back of the van. He flopped over into the driver's seat and shouted for me to get in. "Can you believe this place?" he exclaimed. We've got to get out of here or we may never leave. Can you believe it? That's the way things ought to be. Cork it in a bottle, carve it in sculpture, but keep it!"

Within seconds, still drunk, we had circled the barricades and found the road to Guatemala. Despite our hangovers we turned the volume all the way up on the The Who's history refrain

There'll be fighting in the streets
With our children at our feet,
And the morals that they worshiped
will be gone...

Pick up my guitar and play,
Just like yesterday, and I'll get on my
knees and pray,
We don't get fooled again. No No...

19

Still reeling from the night in Juchitan, we weaved out of the tepid lowlands and into the cooler mountains toward San Cristobal de Las Casas. "Still the old colonial area," I read to Tom. "Large haciendas and peasants toiling for their daily survival."

"Survival, that's not such a bad idea," he analyzed. You know Bro, I kind of like that. These guys just eat a few beans, fuck, do little work and watch the world go by. What else is there in the end. You think those old owners are any happier?"

"Who knows?" Maybe you should ask some of those old revolutionaries."

"Maybe I'll just do that Bro," Tom decided as he pulled into a peasant bar, a pulqueria. "Let's go in here and have a drink."

Inside the EL CUERVO, five peasants dressed in colorful ponchos sat at the narrow bar sipping the putrid pulgue, a sour homebrew beer, from large ceramic mugs. When we walked in the chatter turned silence. The bartender looked at us impassively with cardboard eyes and said nothing.

"Senor," Tom requested. "Cervezas por los hombres." The peasants nodded but didn't push any conversation. In fact, they ignored us.

"Amigos," Tom toasted. "Viva Zapata, Viva la Revolucion." We drank but the men didn't. They turned their heads and began whispering among themselves, drinking sporadically between stares.

"Tom, they don't care," I said. "It's nobody's revolution. We better get out of here. I don't think that they like us or the revolution."

"Oh hell, they ought too," Tom said, shaking my grip from his arm. "Damn, it must have been fun, throwing over the old order, running across the desert and through the mountains taking what should have been yours. What's wrong with these guys?"

"Come on Tom, let's go," I urged, nudging him towards the door.

"Fuck you cowards," Tom yelled in English. "You don't move, you just sit here taking it. What kind of bums are you. Your wives and your children will forget you."

After a struggle, I clothes-lined Tom into the van and he calmed down. Like children listening to a carnival barker, the five peasants stood outside the door watching us. Finally, Tom started the van and we pulled away.

"You know what pissed me off about them, John?" Tom said "They didn't care about anything. They were just there."

"I know," I know."

We passed through San Cristobal and spent the night near the Guatemalan border, crossing over in the morning without any problems, thanks to our letter. On the Mexican side of the border the guard had peered into the van and motioned us to get out. "Your passports," he said in English as he opened Tom's door. Knowing Tom would be driving, I had put the letter in Tom's papers. The guard waved his arm for us to follow him into the border station. His lips were tight and his walk deliberate, as if he already considered us his prisoners. Abruptly, a step before the door, he stopped. He straightened, slowly turning the pages of Tom's passport and burying his eyes in it as if he were studying a Bible. Then he turned and motioned us to stop, waving his hands in front of him like a traffic cop, "Un momento," he said. He went inside and returned in a minute with the captain, an extremely fat man who puffed when he walked. "Come enn, Come enn, our feeds," he squealed, holding open the door for us. We were treated to ham sandwiches and all the cold beer we wanted before we continued on our way. The guards stood outside and waved to us when we left, our dust blowing behind us into their smiling faces as we crossed the border.

The change of scenery was sudden. Long winding waterfalls cascaded down the mountains and clear pools of cool, fresh water was by the roadsides for the traveler's convenience. We stopped at one to wash the hot Isthmus dust from our bodies. While we were bathing, a bus load of Indians stopped on the highway and watched the show. "It must be our whiteness," I told Tom. "Looks like we'll be Barnum and Bailey for a few minutes."

We continued southeast into the mountains until we passed a hunched Indian with an embroidered skirt and a bowler hat. He was toting a heavy-looking load of grass mats on his back. We stopped and bought one for about twenty-five cents and tried to talk with him about the area. But all he understood of Spanish was numbers.

We continued on to Chichicastenango, a mountain town that supposedly retained the flavor of the old Mayan days. It was a clean town with whitewashed walls and the same cool air we had breathed coming through San Cristobal de las Casas. When we arrived, church bells were ringing and the Indians in their colorful woven dresses were scurrying towards the sound. A priest stood on the steps of the old colonial church waving incense, the smoke settling down like mountain mist.

We ate lunch at a local restaurant with an American proprietor whom we asked about the local sights. "Well, it's Sunday," he reflected. "If you like the odd, and you must if you are here, you might like to see the peasants worshipping their idols up on the hill. A few of them will go up there after Mass. But don't get too close. They're a little shy, these Mayas. They might run off."

"We see enough of that in Mexico City," Tom said.

"Not like this," he answered. "These folks can even be funny. Why they even have an idol that when they worship they stick a cigar in its mouth. You never know what you're going to see."

We washed our chicken dinner down with rich highland coffee and proceeded up the hill path the owner had told us about. Like the lifelessness that ran down into the metro in Mexico City, this path wound through several peasant houses. In one, a woman was just completing a tapestry that she held up for our inspection and a hopeful sale. It was a small piece of cloth sewed between two pieces of wood featuring sewn dogs mating. I bought it for about five dollars. "Damn fine piece you've got there" Tom held it up for inspection. "Too bad you didn't have that in college to impress the sorority girls. You could've hung it right over the head of your bed. It'd sure work better than a conquistador mask."

"That's what I plan on doing now." I rolled it up and stuck it in my belt. "The trouble is that this thing may be some sort of fertility charm. And that's not what I need now, a little Mexican kid following me around Disneyland."

The path ended at the edge of a clearing at the hilltop. We heard the chanting and knelt behind some brush as we watched a young Indian woman spray the blood of a freshly decapitated chicken over a black stone with a crude face carved on its surface. Around the stone were black wooden crosses. "Damn, that's not Christian. So why are those crosses there?"

"I think they represent the four directions," I guessed. "And your right, its's not Christian. It's probably from another time."

"Or from this time," he said with assurance.

We went back down the hill and passed a line of Indians making their way up to the idol. "One mass to another," I thought. These people were still yearning for something. I was too, but I wondered about Tom. He had Angie, or thought he did. I wanted to talk with him about it, but I didn't. We had an emotional truce about her. And right now she was gone.

We left the old time religion, skirted Guatemala City and turned on the road to Tikal, the ancient metropolis of the Mayas. It was a bad, narrow road, covered with potholes and rocks. I remembered the Sea Dog's warning and feared Belize if its roads were as bad as this one. It was dangerous, too. I had heard about a former music teacher at the American School who had been shot in the butt while taking a leak on this route, and after what had happened to me in Puerto Escondito, I felt uneasy.

We spent a sleepless night parked in Sebol and bumped into Tikal late on Monday afternoon. It was magnificent! Before London was a village, this place had numbered four-hundred thousand people and its influence had covered the Americas, before they were such. It's ceremonial center rose out of the jungle like rockets pointed at the stars and the lush vegetation covered its dead secrets of daily life.

I strung the hammock, covered myself with a mosquito net and slept under the jungle canopy while Tom slept in the van. The next morning, after visiting the temples along the tourist path, we went to a small spring to bathe. The water was still for a spring and was mucus green with algae. A gangly girl with long twiny blonde hair was bathing there alone. She stood up and smiled, inviting us to join her. "Come on in, the water's fine," she said. "There's no reason to by shy around here."

We splashed and traded recent experinces. "Ecuador, now that's the place to go," she kept repeating. "What a great place, you've just got to go there. Cotopoxie is beautiful and the Indians are so quaint and not spoiled by the tourists like these Mayas." I hated that talk because I didn't want to hear about places I wasn't going to visit. I considered it one-upmanship from the gypsy brigade. I wanted to hear about places where we were and places where tourist hadn't been.

"And by the way," she asked, finally giving us a chance to talk. "Didn't you say you were teaching in Mexico City?" Well, a friend of mine who lives near me in New York said if I went through there I should call a fellow named Tom who works at some American school. You guys know him?"

Tom and I shot each other looks of total surprise. "He's him," I said pointing at Tom.

"Well I'll be damned," she exclaimed. "What a coincidence. I guess some things are just meant to be, aren't they. I mean, after all, that's what the old Aztecs believed and now that I'm beginning to understand more of..."

That night was an eclipse of the moon. Tom, the girl and I

climbed the tallest temple we could find and waited as the moon slowly crossed the scene below. From another temple the sound of a flute shrilled over the jungle and appeared to come from everywhere. "Years ago, they would be cutting our hearts out here," I said.

"Doesn't matter," Tom said softly. "I've lost it plenty of other ways."

"I wish I was here years ago," the girl said. "I wouldn't have minded being sacrificed because it was the high point of their lives."

"Please be quite for just a minute," I pleaded. "Let us enjoy this." The girl pulled up her knees and looked towards the dying moon.

Below, the monkeys screamed. The wind blew and the fragile trees swung nervously as the light disappeared in a hurricane of darkness. Then the wind ceased and it was as if it were the beginning or the end of time, and everything was lost within itself. Then slowly the light returned, revealing creation in a steady rhythm across the face of the earth.

"Welcome back to the world, Bro," Tom said, breaking our religious silence. "And you too, sweetheart."

We climbed down and returned to the campground and civilization. The girl toddled along after Tom and they slept together in the van beneath Tom's battery-powered fan. I slept in my hammock dreaming to the returning sounds of life.

I woke to an erie morning with a canopy of mist settling into the jungle. The monkey chatter had stopped. They were probably sleeping after their apocalypse the previous night.

Tom and the girl were sitting in the door of the van and drinking cokes. The girl was smoking a joint. "I guess I might come and see you in Mexico City," she said to Tom.

"That's not such a good idea," he responded. "I'm living with someone right now."

"Well, give me a ring back home when she moves out. I kind of like it down here. I'll stay with you awhile and then go back to Ecuador, OK."

"OK," Tom said, folding her address and phone number and shoving the paper into the van's glove compartment.

By mid-morning we were on the way to Belize. To survive the heat, we only wore our underwear and a loose shirt. We were out of ice and the beer was warm. "You know Bro, I could've stayed at that temple all night," Tom said. I felt like that old moon was just going to suck me right up."

"Yeah," I said. "Maybe that's where we belong these days, on top of some temple watching the moon die and being reborn."

I took a last swallow of tepid beer and silently wished for a heaven of ice, a place somewhere soon down the road, while Credence reminded me of the hot, Tikal moon:

> *I see a bad moon a risen.*
> *I see trouble on the way.*
> *I see earthquakes and lighting,*
> *I see bad times a day.*
> *Don't go round tonight,*
> *It's bound to take your life.*
> *There's a bad moon on the rise.*

20

Through the morning we traveled the gravelly road, surrounded on both sides with jungle growth until we reached the border station on the Guatemalan border. We were the only souls moving on the road and when we arrived at the crossing, all three of the guards, black as night and speaking the Queen's Island English, came out to meet us. "Didn't you know Mon, that you just came through a military zone?" One of the guards pointed out to us casually. "The Guatemalans have troops and tanks over there waiting to attack us. They want our country but are afraid of our Mother Queen. She still loves us. We still have her picture on all of our money!" The guard pulled out his wallet and showed us that every denomination of bill had the portrait of Her Majesty.

Tom and I presented our passports for inspection but the guard didn't appear interested. Instead, he asked us how much money we had. We showed him the three-hundred dollars we had between us. "That's not enough, Mon," he said shaking his head. You must have one-thousand dollars each to come into our country. We don't allow hippies here, only good citizens with money." Tom pointed to the letter in his passport. "I don't read Spanish Mon, only English and Creole."

"OOOh man," Tom whined, giving the guard his best "aw shucks" expression. "You know we don't have that much money in cash, but we may have something that's worth that much." Tom picked up his cassette case from behind the seat and began to thumb through his tapes. The guards crowded around his door trying to read the titles. Tom's racing fingers stopped on a Johnny Mathis tape. "You guys like Johnny Mathis?" Tom asked. "You know this tape is worth a lot of money."

The guard lifted the tape from the case and then quickly took the *BEATLES WHITE ALBUM* along with it. My face fell. It was one of our favorites. We had listened to *Revolution* while passing through every poor village in Mexico. His fingers didn't stop there. Since there were three guards our entrance fee was three tapes. I tried not to show my heartsickness when he chose *WHO'S NEXT*. The agents quickly stamped our passports and slipped a three-week visa into them. "Have fun friends," he called as we drove into Belize.

It wasn't long before we discovered that Belize was a citadel of capitalism. There were only two beers in this country and they were involved in an advertising war. The first billboard read:

BELICAN (PICTURE OF A LOVELY WHITE COUPLE)
THE ONLY BEER WORTH DRINKING

We soon climbed from the steamy lowlands into the mountains and we stopped briefly to dip in a mountain stream. Except for the black family bathing upstream from us, we could've been in Montana. It felt good to lie in the cool rushing water while it washed dirt from our bodies. It was the first really clean water we had bathed in since we cruised into Guatemala.

By late afternoon we reached Belize City and I immediately fell in love with this pirate town. Its narrow streets were full of white-gloved policemen waving crowded traffic by without any thought or attention. They could have been directing a bed of angry ants. And the streets were crowded with a zoo of people: Mennonites, completely clothed in their orthodox garments; Texas cowboys in their hats, here for the cheap land; and ragged blacks, who lived in the mahogany shacks on the edge of the town. The blacks were riding bicycles, the Mennonites were walking and the cowboys were driving trucks. It was a glorious mess.

We pulled into Lucy's cafe near the fish market and ordered a Texas-styled hamburger. We could smell the thick saltfish air from our table. I stared out the window at this Caribbean old world and wondered if this was my place, a kind of buffer zone of time where I could climb back into the past with less danger than in Mexico.

We spent the night in the town's only campground and arose early the next day. By eight o'clock we had eaten breakfast at Lucy's, read a creole newspaper with the headlines *DE KNEW BARGE SINK*, and located a lumber boat that would take us to Cay Caulker on the edge of the barrier reef to do some snorkeling. We had heard about the beauty of the reef and were eager to see it before the travel agencies got there with all of their accountant customers. I knew it wouldn't be long.

The boat was loaded with lumber down below, but it had a small upper deck with a few lounge chairs for passengers. We were the only ones. As we putted towards Cay, I thought about the Smartest Man in the World. I could see him, an apparition from the narrow past, still banging his soundless keys to a ghostly melody heard only by his own soul.

"Beautiful place," Tom mused, looking back across the azure water toward the coast. "I'll bet this is as close as we'll be to seeing what ole Columbus saw when he hit this place."

"Columbus didn't know where the hell he was," I reminded Tom. "He lived in a world of his own imagination, and then he was lucky that it coincided with reality."

"Still, he had impressions," Tom added. "He had to know. He had to know!"

"I still admire Cortez more," I argued. "He was reality and seized it, and he knew it. Columbus didn't know because he didn't have the guts to let go."

"Well Bro, then I'm more like Columbus because I'll never let it go either. It goes where I go," he said softly.

We arrived at Cay Caulker late that morning. It looked like the desolate island joke of some cartoon. We took our bags and walked up the Island path past a few stilted houses until we reached the one that said *HOTEL*. A young black man sitting on the veranda motioned us inside. There was no office, but two rooms were reserved for tourists. We were the only guests. Our room had two cots, a rotating fan and no decorations. It was the bottom line.

There were no restaurants on the Cay so we ate lunch at a family's house that advertised meals for tourists. We paid five dollars each for green beans, onions and chicken poured out of English cans. Crates of canned food were even used for furniture. The proprietor was an older, two-hundred pound white woman from Michigan who was married to a younger, slim, native black man. It took her ten minutes to heat up our meal on the stove.

That afternoon we found the local tourist center. Gil, the guide, was a middle-aged salt who took the Cay's occasional tourist to the reef. His enterprise consisted of an eighteen-foot aluminum skiff, rental snorkeling gear and an air compressor. A fish lunch, prepared by a black teen, was included with the price of the trip. "If you don't like the meal," he told us, "let me know and I'll get another girl next time I go to Belize. Hell, there's plenty of 'um just dying to be domestic. Anyway, they get old in a hurry." The girl kept her distance from Gil except to serve him. Her face was neutral, expressionless, and I never saw her blink. "She's really not so bad you know, in some ways." Gil wiped his hands on his white tee shirt and waited for a response, but we ignored the gesture. We just wanted to hurry and get to the reef.

Gil putted the skiff with his twenty-five horse Johnson to the edge of the reef. Tom and I slid into the clear water and an instant look at a rainbow world. Multi-colored tropical fish darted into honeycombs or coral, peering back out at us from their rooms. Some swam swiftly toward us, protecting their domains by attacking our arms and legs and not ceasing until we moved away.

However much I admired the little fish, I still wanted to kill the big ones. I speared a grouper and held it up for Tom's inspection when we surfaced. His face contorted like an infant's in pain. He swan back to the boat and threw his rented gun on board. "I just can't shoot them," he said. "I just can't."

At sunset we returned to Gil's where his girl cooked the grouper I had killed. Tom wouldn't eat any and settled for a can of Vienna sausages and beans.

"You boys care for any recreation," Gil asked after we finished eating. "It's cheap."

"You got bowling alley's on this Island?" Tom asked, knowing damn well what Gil meant.

Gil pulled a rusty bread box out of the kitchen cabinet and cut several lines of cocaine on the smooth wooden table. "Stuff's cheap here, and nobody gives a damn," he said as we snorted our lines through plastic straws. It was my second time. Of course, I had seen the stuff being used in drug abuse films they showed us in high school. In those, some poor girl usually snorted and then let the whole football team gang bang her, then she woke up, discovered her addiction and committed suicide by snorting a bushel and driving her car into a nursery school bus, maiming everyone on board. I was afraid of the stuff and its charge, but I was in the mood and it did me right. It gave me the same feeling I had when I first entered the water that afternoon, a feeling of clarity and euphoria.

"It'll make the girl look prettier, and she's worth a little money," Gil said. "Girl, come here." She came over to the table and stood between me and Tom. "Go ahead, grab her ass, it's nice and round." Despite the cocaine rush, I couldn't, and neither could Tom. We sat still, embarrassed. Gil grabbed the girl's dress and pulled her to him. He cut a few more lines and they finished them without sharing. "Just trying to run a little business boys," he said, more as a statement than an apology.

Still flushed from the coke, we spent the remainder of the evening at the Cay's only bar. We downed Gallo, the "only beer worth drinking" and watched a crooked and grey-haired old black man dance to island music and the light of the moon. A bearded American fellow with hair down his back and a moonscape face stood near us, but he didn't speak. On his shoulders was a black kid who bounced his feet against the American's chest in time with the music. We left the American alone. At least I had learned that much.

We enjoyed ourselves until the no-see'ums, those dreadful little flies that penetrate the skin like hypodermic needles, began to attack. But the old man kept dancing as if his steps were a response to the pain.

Drunk and exhausted, we returned to our hotel near midnight and tried to crash in our bunks, but as soon as I felt myself drifting to sleep, the fan stopped. "Damn," Tom cursed after a few minutes of suffering the no-see'ums and the heat. "This place is run on generators and I'll bet they cut them after midnight, shit."

After fifteen minutes or so we decided to escape outside to the porch, but it didn't work. There was no breeze. We tried the bar but it was no better. The old man was still there asleep against the wall.

From there we wandered to the windward beach of the Cay. Here, the breeze repelled our tormentors, but it was high tide and the water had claimed most of the sand and left us only with the island graveyard fronting the water. Its stones were turned at different angles from years of storms and it looked as if the second coming had occurred, leaving us alone to ponder our sins. Tom and I chose our stones, stretching out on them and sleeping until dawn. When I awoke I read my redeemer's name:

RUFUS DUNWOODY
BORN AUGUST 29, 1945
DIED JULY 3, 1968

WE REMEMBER HIM
YOU DON'T

But Tom's stone had been faded by more years of sun, sand and storms. It was almost smooth and without an identity, except for the irregular pattern that clashed together like the lines in the palm of a hand. Tom was affected by his bed. He sat on his haunches in a meditative pose, breaking twigs with his fingers and contemplating the stone's surface as if he were waiting for the name's appearance. "I wonder who it was," he said.

"Does it matter? He was here when you needed him."

"Or her," he said.

After dawn, we ate breakfast at the house and asked what time the boat back to Belize City came. "Oh Mon, about three weeks," the chef answered.

"Man, we've got to be back in Mexico City in less than a week," I pointed out. "How can we get off this damn island?"

"Oh Mon, there's lumber boat sometime, maybe tonight. Maybe if you stay up you find one. They go market. They bring us lumber, take back fish traps. But we don't know when they come. Could be anytime, could be month."

We sat out in the graveyard until we got lucky. One came at three o'clock the next morning. It was a long ride back. Water sloshed around my feet and every time my head nodded to my chest I startled awake. Tom didn't fare any better. The gas fumes made him weak, so he never slept but stared ahead across the moonlit water, waiting to arrive.

The return road did nothing to belie the warning of the Oaxaca seer. The road wasn't very old, but it had been built by the British before they forced independence on Belize, and it hadn't been repaired in years, leaving concrete holes and ruts with jagged edges that slowed the van down to under twenty kilometers per hour. We were bumped and thrown like bowling pins and our nerves jangled like loose change. Still in Belize, we passed Mayan ruins reclaimed by the jungle, now nappy mounds of grass sprouting small, knotty trees.

By evening we reached the Mexican border. Once again, we had no trouble crossing because of our letter. Once again, we were treated to beer and a meal. We spent the night in the van and continued on the next day to Palenque, but I had lost my interest in ruins. I showered in the park restrooms while Tom visited some king's tomb. He was interested in the carving, but I didn't want to hear about it. There had to be something in this country besides ruins. I thought it might be a good idea to raze them and build something new, but then the rubble must be cleared away first. It wasn't worth the trouble.

We travelled through the province of Tabasco, where Graham Green's priest had stumbled around, and then on past the grimy, sulfuric oil fields, Mexico's monuments to glut, and into Veracruz where we spent the night swatting mosquitoes the size of sparrows. Cortez, I remembered, had began his conquest here. We continued to follow his route past the Pico de Orizaba and the city of Puebla. I had seen Puebla's morning lights when I had climbed Popo, blinking on and off like stars appearing from behind clouds. Then it had seemed innocent and new with potential, another world. Now in the heat it seemed so old, its life burned out, and light was only the sun's punishment, magnifying its decay. We passed the cathedral where Tom and Angie had once mentioned getting married, as if it were possible, and then took the road back to Mexico City. We rode in silence.

21

At first, there was only a daily drizzle that temporarily cleansed the poisonous haze from the valley of Mexico, but by June's end the turbulent afternoon thunderstorms of the rainy season had created transitory rivers that swept cars from the roads and left a slippery algae slime on the city's sidewalks.

Angie returned from Minnesota and since the Oaxaca rescue, my relationship with Tom and her had improved. She became more of a quarrelsome sister than a lethal tigress. She felt her hold on Tom was secure. I had been defeated and I knew it, so now I was acceptable and could even be used if the situation presented itself. I knew my space and I was happy there because I had control.

McNapp continued to enjoy our company and insisted on treating us to expensive meals in Lomas and the Zona Rosa. He developed a fondness for Popo Red and spent many weekend hours stoned, staring blankly at our Indian blanket walls as if he were contemplating making larger welcome mats for a market of giants.

We threw a couple of parties and McNapp presided over them like a happy grandfather at a holiday dinner, providing all the booze and dope for the revelers. The guests at these parties weren't people we knew very well, just travelers we had met in the Zona Rosa or other foreigners I had encountered at the language school. Ralfe, the philosophy teacher and his gay friends, were there along with their female companion, a porno movie director from L.A. She beat the gays in the bathroom and they crawled down the stairs on their hands and knees whimpering. We laughed at the show.

Alone, McNapp usually sat on the stairs, cigarette clutched between his fingers, silently observing. I wondered what happened to my prostitute scouting trip and still savored visions of gorgeous girls dancing down stairs and the men saluting with wine glasses to the one with the highest kick, or the best tits.

Tilly was a different story. She avoided our house and kept her distance at school, making only small talk over a quick cup of coffee or orange juice and keeping her advice secured in her own piggy bank, stashed away for future use.

On the last afternoon of June 20, McNapp telephoned. "Come over now, you and Tom and the girl," he ordered. There was fear in his voice. I had never mentioned the night we left the no-name whorehouse so quickly, but his emergency tone of voice was the same as if something, a poltergeist, was emerging from a forbidden grave to grab him, some sort of resurrected Mexican god.

Tom and I arrived at his house on Calle Amsterdam about thirty minutes later. He was sitting by the phone in his living room with photos and a brown paper bag scattered in front of him. His eyes were blinking quickly, his trait of true worry. He motioned us to the couch. "I need you to be with me tonight mates. Don't have any other plans. I think I'll need you to go some place with me. I'm waiting now to see."

"What's wrong, your help quit at Happy's McNapp," joked Tom.

McNapp ignored the humor. "I need you to see some things mates," he said. "And hear some things. You are my friends, right?" I don't believe it ever entered his mind that we might not believe him, that he might just be putting a notary stamp on his own records by telling us his own rhetorical history.

He answered the phone on the first ring. "Yeah, um huh. Yeah, I heard from him earlier. What do you want me to do here. Um huh. I'll take care of it. You'll hear from me later, when it's all done." He hung up. "Sam's dead," he said turning to us. "Sam Giancano. He was assassinated last night while cooking sausages in his basement. The bastards."

Tom and I looked at McNapp quizzically. We don't normally ask him about his life but this time he was begging the questions. He had something he wanted to tell us that was paining him like a rock in his shoe, and he had to empty it.

"Who's Sam," I asked.

"Sam's dead," he repeated. "The man who had Kennedy shot. My boss and friend. He's a very important Chicago businessman."

I would have laughed if McNapp hadn't been so scared. He dropped his lighter twice before lighting his cigarette and his hands shook like an old man's. "There are some things I think you should know in case something happens to me. And there are some things I want to show you," he replied, as if to convince himself about his decision.

We all sat quietly. He wasn't asking for a response. I sensed Tom and Angie were thinking the same thing: that McNapp was crazy, suffering from delusions, paranoia, schizophrenia, in other words, twentieth-century sick. But the shock of this improbable story rendered us powerless to challenge.

McNapp sensed our doubts. "Come over here," he said. "I have a collection of mementoes."

On the table were several pictures. In one photo two well-dressed attractive men, one older, one younger, had their arms around McNapp at a well-set restaurant table. They looked drunk. The photo was a dull black and white, a Polaroid anachronism, like an old K-Mart ten-for-a-dollar-shot. "That's Sam and Dick with me in Chicago. Dick was Sam's and my best friend." McNapp pointed to the younger man. The photo showed a squared chin and deep set eyes. "Dick ran Sam's interest here in Mexico City. Damn, he was a fine fellow. Brilliant you know. A real intellectual. And he was my friend. He's dead now. Somebody blew the back of his head off with a shotgun in a Chicago cafe. Sam said this was the gun he was carrying when he was killed. He gave it to me as a present. Don't ask me why but they do those kinds of things. I guess it's their way of being sentimental."

McNapp reached into the brown paper sack and brought out a .45 caliber Smith & Wesson. "I know it's morbid son-of-a-bitch, but it does remind me of things." McNapp placed the gun on the table. "Now I represent Sam in Mexico," he said, almost as an afterthought. "That's important, you know, because he had to leave suddenly last year. I'm not sure I know what to do now. There is a lot involved."

"What about the Kennedy thing," I asked nonchalantly. "What's the story?"

"He crossed'um," McNapp began. "They were his friends and he crossed'um. He and Sam shared the same woman. And then he went after'um with that son-of-a-bitch little brother of his. He got political and forgot his friends. It was easy to arrange down here at the Cuban embassy. Sam and his mates had contacts."

"So the Cubans had Oswald kill Kennedy. And it was arranged by Sam?" Tom questioned.

"No, the Cubans had nothing to do with it," McNapp corrected. "But it was easy to arrange. They made a convenient alibi, that's all." McNapp quit confessing and we didn't ask for more. If he was mad we didn't want to encourage him, especially me. I had seen the deep look he now had before, and it showed something besides friendship, something lost or distant inside those windows to his soul. "Come on, let's go in your van," McNapp directed. "I have some people to see."

It occurred to me that he wanted us along to protect him, but he didn't even take the .45 beside him. Besides, what could we do? No, he wanted witnesses. Perhaps he was afraid he would vanish and his history would become invisible, except as a footnote in the archives of the empire to the north.

Within a few hours McNapp's spurious connections were as valid as a ticket to an underground parking lot. First, we visited several of Mexico City's best restaurants, including the one where I had eaten with McNapp before we went to the politicians whorehouse. Of course, we went there also.

Next, we headed down to the Zona Rosa and hit several places including our beloved El Vaso de Oro. Between stops, McNapp had Tom drive a circuitous path around the city, once even passing the luminous ape on Los Ninos Periditos. At each place the procedure was the same: a well-dressed Latin, probably the owner, met McNapp at the door and escorted us to an office or a back room. Here, the gentleman said a few words to McNapp about our "Compadre," toasted a glass of red wine, and then passed a sealed envelope to him. Then, McNapp handed the envelope to Tom or me. "Keep these on you," were his only instructions. The host usually glanced at us with scared cat-eyes. McNapp simply assured the host with a "mis amigos." Finally, we drank a final toast to the deceased and ate an appetizer: another sacrifice for the dead. I felt we were entering some pagan church community, celebrating a mass as obscure as an Aztec ritual. It was too bad Tom couldn't buy a mask to commemorate the occasion.

At the El Vaso de Oro there was one more guest in the office: the Colonel. He was dressed in a dark blue suit and his sunglasses were off, revealing milky grey eyes. "I see you made it boys. Welcome to Mexico," he said. We shook hands, and his were dry and grainy, like parched sand on the beach. "I hope you're not surprised I'm here," he continued. "You see, I have a talent for, let's say, getting people together to solve mutual needs. That sort of thing. I'm glad you came along. We need you."

McNapp accepted an envelope from the owner and another one from the Colonel while we drank the inevitable toast. Truthfully, I wasn't surprised to see the Colonel. A strange man in a strange country during a strange time. It all fit. A man without a country, without a time, without an identity, he could be very valuable to somebody.

"You know, it's too bad we didn't succeed with that Castro thing," the Colonel said to McNapp as we got up to leave. "You think that had something to do with it?"

"No," McNapp replied. "That pill thing with Orselli and Harvey was nothing, just smoke. They were afraid of the big one, mate. When he left last year we knew it was going to happen sooner or later. It had too. We had lost control. The protection had broken down."

"Well, on to bigger and better things," the Colonel toasted us as we left the office. "Enjoy the rest of your stay in Mexico, boys."

We left the El Vaso de Oor and walked into the wet streets. It was after ten o'clock and the night chill hung over the city with the same ferocity as the afternoon's pollution. "Take a taxi to the airport," McNapp instructed us. "At the Texas International ticket counter there will be a tall American wearing white slacks and a tourist shirt with *ACULPULCO* printed all over it. Your names are Sam, Dick and Ruth. His is Eric. He'll take the envelopes. Act like he's your long lost travelling buddy. I'll drive the van and meet you at your place later."

McNapp walked off toward the van and left us to flag down our own taxi. We never thought to question his plans. We were on automatic pilot and like most people, the zombies of history, shuffling along, our senses dead to seminal events, or even to the yield signs of the past.

The taxi ride was almost silent and even Angie was at a loss for words. We were slightly drunk from the night's wine toasts. The only conversation was small talk about the tourists whose roles we were playing. Tom was the caretaker of the envelopes and he fingered them nervously, as if they were Sunday School bulletins in the hands of a child waiting for the sermon to end. Our eyes converged on them with fear and worship, as if we were witnessing a saint's apparition delivering a message from the Almighty.

When we approached the airport, I leaned over the front seat and instructed the driver to circle around the airport three times before he let us off. "There may be someone following us," I explained to Tom and Angie, even though I knew I was lying. What I really wanted was to stall, put off the inevitable involvement.

"I know," Tom said.

Angie looked out the rear window. For several blocks she watched intently, not talking or moving, or even blinking her eyes. Occasional street lamps painted jagged light puzzle patterns over her face. "There's nobody back there," she said.

There was no trouble at the airport. We met McNapp's contact who greeted us and called us by our appointed names. He pumped our hands, hugged Angie, and led us to the bar where Tom passed him the envelopes. It was all very cordial. We could have been distant kin exchanging souvenirs. We kept up the charade until the fictitious friend walked through the international gate on the way to his late-night plane. We even waved good-bye.

McNapp never returned to his house. Early the next morning he took a taxi to Cuernervaca. "Don't go to Happy's anymore," he cautioned us before he left. "I won't have anything more to do with it and you shouldn't be seen there. My business is elsewhere now. I'll call you soon."

22

School came to an end in July. Angie and I signed contracts for the coming year, but Tom resigned before they could refuse to offer him one. Instead, he was going to teach English to adults at a part-time language school. Tom was never one for structure. At the adult school he could set his own hours and travel more often, perhaps even spending some time in that South American monolith. Also, he was beginning to work more on his own sculpture. In the past few months he had constructed three contemporary pieces out of thrown-away metal and wood scraps. He got the idea one day when we saw a poor Mexican scurrying down the street with a broken guitar neck, its strings still attached and waving like the Medusa's snake hair. Tom connected those scraps with wire and worked them into an oval shape with space inside the borders and called it *GARBAGE WITH A FOUNDATION*. "You see, Bro," he explained. "The wood and metal will slowly decompose and show its age. That's what'll make the piece, the change. It will create itself."

None of us went home that summer. Instead, digested the unique events of the past month over Bohemias, pot and for Angie and Tom, a snowstorm of cocaine. We decided McNapp was a trusted friend who was making us his special protectors because he trusted our homespun innocence. After all, we were safe friends who had nothing to gain from him but a good time and lots of interesting stories. We didn't take him too seriously, at least not at first. We felt no sense of immediate danger, but rather a fractured sense of contemporary history. We knew something we thought few people knew, a spider's web of myth that was being revealed from a dark closet and were impressed with our own uniqueness as confidants.

"I can remember exactly what I was doing the day Kennedy was shot," I reminisced one morning over breakfast at Sanborn's.

"Everybody does John, that's the American cliche," Angie reminded me.

"But we remember it because our actions tell us something about ourselves," I continued.

"OK, tell us your story," Angie conceded. "We're going to hear about it sooner or later anyway."

"My sixth grade teacher came into our class after lunch crying and told us the President had been shot," I began. "We cheered. We hated him, or thought we did because of all that crap about integration. He was a Yankee picking on the South, telling the world about the "nigger" problem in Birmingham. We wanted to fight the Civil War all over again. After school that day, we rode a bus to play YMCA flag football against Vernor Elementary. We shouted and waved out the windows little Confederate flags we had made out of colored paper. We won the game. I made an eighty-yard touchdown run."

"God, how morbid," Angie reacted. "You Southerners are unbelievable. How could you feel like that. That makes you part of the murder. You're as much killers as Lee Harvey Oswald." She tossed her long black hair to the side in a gesture of disgust.

"We didn't know," I explained. We thought we were defending our territory. The Kennedys were hurting us by trying to send the "blacks" to our schools. We were raised hearing about the Southern way of life and they were destroying it. At least that's what we thought. We believed our parents."

"Well, I wasn't around for any public demonstrations that day," Tom included. "I was cutting school at Lynda's house and we were screwing on the floor. The radio announcement interrupted Elvis and us."

"And I guess you were mad about that," Angie hissed.

"Yeah, I was, a little. "But what the hell do you know," Tom replied angrily. "I don't have to be ashamed. As a matter of fact, my father was a newspaper man who supported the Civil rights movement. Crosses were burned on our yard and I was beaten up at school more than once. We had our lives threatened over the phone and eventually my father had to quit. He never recovered. He began doing odd things, like growing marijuana in flower pots and driving trucks that were loaded with contraband bananas from Honduras. Finally, he went too far. He killed himself in 1969 by drinking Tylenol, and leaving the world's shortest legal will: Everything wife."

"Tom, I'm sorry. Why didn't you tell me?" Angie asked.

"Because it wouldn't have done any good. And besides, you didn't need to know," Tom answered. "After all, I'm his living example going backwards. All I need to do now is to find a great failure."

Tom had never told me this story either, but I had guessed something akin to tragedy. We had both left out pieces of our lives when we talked, but like spaces of a missing puzzle, we could see the whole from the missing pattern. They showed the glimpses of truth, whatever that was those days.

Later that night came McNapp's promised call. He was in Cuernervaca and wanted us to come and stay with him a few days. "I have a business proposition for you," he told Tom. "And bring Angie and John too. They can help. Be here in the morning."

At nine, we arrived at McNapp's. He lived about three blocks from the Zocalo in a modern Spanish-style one-story stucco house with mahogany doors and window frames. There was an acre yard complete with gardens, fruit trees and an Olympic-sized swimming pool bordered by Mexican tiles in the front. The only unsettling aspect of this property was the prison towers that rose above the walls to the north.

"Make yourselves at home," McNapp greeted us, sweeping his arms towards the pool with a Columbus-style gesture as if he were showing us his new world. "I don't really like the place, but it makes my friends comfortable and my wife likes it. She'll be coming back from Europe in August."

We squeezed fresh limes from McNapp's trees and drank cool green Margaritas over crushed ice while we drifted on rafts in the pool and listened to Pink Floyd's *DARK SIDE OF THE MOON*. McNapp sat like a medieval lord in a lounge chair and watched us. Every now and then he contributed bits and pieces of trivial conversation, but nothing proportional to the earthquake revelations of our last meeting. He seemed content to watch us float while he wrote long letters to his missing wife.

After his servants brought us lunch, Tom and Angie did a few lines of McNapp's prime Columbian coke and retired to their bedroom, leaving McNapp alone with me. "I'll be honest with you, mate", he said while I fixed another margarita and passed him a joint. "This proposal I spoke of mainly concerns Tom and Angie. I won't really need you, but I know Tom will feel more comfortable if you're involved in some way."

"But McNapp," I protested childishly. "I thought we were friends." I was hurt because I felt I had shared more good time with McNapp than Tom or Angie, especially while they were lost in their world of two.

"Don't take it personally," he responded cooly. "Tom will be a better businessman than you will. He has more to gain and nothing to lose. You have too many other connections. You'll go back someday, I know that. But Tom needs something and I need someone on whom I can depend at any time, someone more free than you who can move around the country."

"And Angie."

"I need her to make an impression," he answered.

"In what way," I asked.

"You'll see."

That night McNapp took us to eat and talk business at Harry's Bar and Grill, the popular place for the rich foreign clientele in

Cuernervaca. Across the Zocalo from the restaurant was Cortez's summer palace, where he came to escape the hassles of Mexico City. I heard that the only statue of him in all of Mexico is in there, but I never went to see it. Truthfully, I never liked statues. Their molded rigidity halts time and their feet are not grounded in the living, moving world. Ole Cortez had been a mover, pushing from the world what he perceived as his just rewards and I was afraid the statue would be his memory's final death.

We ate an American-styled steak dinner and McNapp made his presentation. "Tom, I want you to help me in the silver business," he suggested. "I have people in the north who will supply us with all the turquoise I need cheaply. I want some Indian craftsmen around Taxco to make silver and turquoise custom jewelry. That stuff is going over big in the States these days. You're an artist. I need you to design it for me. Angie can assist you."

"Damn McNapp, this sounds great," Tom was clearly excited. "But what's the deal? Is this a job or what?"

McNapp lifted a thousand-dollar bill from his shirt pocket and placed it in front of him. "This is good faith money. I don't know how much we can make, but I'll give you twenty-percent of every shipment to the States. I'll arrange all the paperwork, transportation problems and business contacts. All you have to do is advise and deliver. I'll take care of all your expenses between shipments. And, of course, all our transactions will be in cash." McNapp crossed his arms on the table and leaned slightly toward Tom.

"Where in the States," Tom asked. "And how."

"Different places," McNapp answered. "New Orleans, Chicago, Boston, New York, Las Vegas, everywhere I have contacts. We'll stay in touch through my people. If there's any problem, phone John or Angie in Mexico City first and then they'll contact me. I don't like to handle problems directly, mate."

"And what'll they get out of this," Tom asked, obviously concerned about our welfare.

McNapp reached back into his shirt pocket and handed Angie

and me each a five-hundred dollar bill. "Like I said, Angie will help design the jewelry and John is a contact, a sort of agent, OK? I'll take care of them including fringe benefits."

Tom glanced at us for any signs of disapproval, but found none. I felt my face flush with excitement and Angie answered with her giggling smile. "Let's get started," Tom said, and then we shook hands all around and sealed the deal with shots of Tequila Sauza, lime and salt.

"Oh, one more little thing," McNapp added. "Tom, you've got to live here with me when you're in Mexico. Of course, Angie and John can come down any time, but I need you here as much as possible. And I'll need Angie here for a couple of weeks to get started, OK?"

"No problem with me. OK with you?" Tom asked us.

"You bet," Angie replied.

"OK" I agreed.

"Waiter, champagne," McNapp called. "We have something to celebrate."

After supper McNapp took us to a house in the Las Quintas neighborhood. "I've got to check up on a few things," he informed us. We stopped at a solid metal gate set in a stone wall facing the street. The doors were smooth and black and appeared to be one piece, like bank vaults. Electrified wires stretched along the foot-thick wall top and like blades of grass on a well-cut lawn, a bed of sharp metal points stuck up through its surface, inviting trespassers to a death by impaling.

McNapp unlocked the gate and we entered a small courtyard. "This was Sam's place while he lived here in Mexico. Nice, isn't it? It even has a name: San Cristobal. I'm in charge of keeping the place up."

Inside, the house had Mexican tile floors and archways over the doors. Small sets of stairs led to certain rooms giving the mansion a split-level feel. Statues of saints and Mary, similar to the ones sold in La Lagunilla, only larger, were spaced around the house, but the most interesting item was an ancient juke-box loaded with Frank Sinatra records. It seemed like heresy among the other decor. "Sam liked juke-boxes," McNapp reminisced. "He got his start with those, ya know."

McNapp called a meeting of the maids and house staff, all five of them. He spoke in rapid Spanish, dismissed them and then turned to us. "I don't really know what to do with this place," he said sadly. "Sam had to leave Mexico kind of suddenly last year. In fact, the Mexican bastards threw him out, the traitors, and now, well, let's just say I don't have any instructions. I imagine some Mexican bastard will claim it if they can get it away from me. You got any ideas?"

"You could turn it into a convent. Put some hymns on that old box and the sisters would feel right at home," Tom suggested.

"Strange, he was quite a religious fellow," McNapp said thoughtfully. "He even gave money to the church, more than I'll ever see. I don't see anything in it myself, but it must've worked for him, for a little while at least."

On the ride back Angie seemed worried. "McNapp, this jewelry thing is legit, I mean..."

McNapp stopped her with his eagle stare. "Yes, of course. Every business I'm involved in is legitimate. You watched too many movies back there in the States. After all, there's nothing wrong with making money and helping friends, like you."

23

We spent the next week working, or at least Tom and Angie did. They worked around the pool using a drafting pad and an assortment of pens and pencils. I had never seen Tom so serious. He spent hours drawing, erasing and cocking his head from side to side to view his work from different perspectives, and after he completed a draft, Angie made her criticisms. "It's the parallax view that counts with jewelry, Tom," she kept repeating. "Jewelry must never look the same from any two perspectives." Angie was covered with jingling, new trinkets, complimentary gifts from new admirers and her white skin had tanned, giving her the appearance of an Aztec princess tempting her warrior into immortality.

I was never asked to comment, which was just as well. For jewelry or sculpture I had no vision and I failed to see the balance, the symmetry. So I spent most of my time reading, drinking and walking the streets of this old colonial paradise. Sometimes in the afternoons I got good and drunk and enjoyed standing by the avocado trees in McNapp's back yard and staring down the prison guards in their towers. I wondered how many American were in there. McNapp had told me that Sam had spent his last night in Mexico there, a captive of those "ungrateful bastards." It couldn't be that bad in there. This was a perfect climate and the prison was small.

Night was party time. McNapp usually invited over a few business friends whom he introduced by their first names: Antonio, Felipe, Joe, et cetera and he never invited any women, just a few chosen prostitutes. His friends were young, attractive and gaudy, usually wearing gold jewelry and silky, luminous shirts that shimmered like the lights on a whorehouse dancefloor. They spoke

English well and casually discussed their visits to faraway places. "We were working together to set up some new businesses with Sam," McNapp explained. "These fellows had some new ideas for the new times."

In addition to the omnipresent marijuana, prime Columbian cocaine was served from gold snuff boxes and snorted lavishly, especially by Angie. Her lines vanished like white highway marks under a car speeding into the night. She usually saw the sunrise of those clear valley mornings. Tom was more cautious. "Can't handle the blues," he told McNapp. "Got to work tomorrow."

McNapp never took any and neither did I. He usually just smoked some grass, surveyed the scene and enjoyed being the host. I didn't take any because I was afraid. I had taken it only twice, a rent snort from one of our many houseguests and on Cay Caulker, and it was too gratifying, almost like a orgasmic afterglow, or even like a little piece of heaven, this Tara of the drug market inhaled with the wind. I knew anything this good had to be bad. I could lose myself and never be found, not even go looking, Besides, I needed pain. Sometimes I think I even enjoyed it. I was beginning to feel it gave me emotional direction and drove me over the rocks and up to Popo's peak.

The next week McNapp, Tom and Angie went to Taxco and travelled into the mountains to contract silversmiths. I invited Lupita down from Mexico City to keep me company. I didn't care for McNapp's prostitutes any more. In fact, I hadn't taken any of them at the nightly get-togethers and McNapp appeared annoyed. He didn't mention my playing Kit Carson for him again.

Lupita and I spent the mornings in bed, the afternoons swimming nude in the pool and the nights at Harry's drinking Beaujolals and reading. For a while, it was all on McNapp.

Tom and Angie returned at the week's end elated about their excursions and their new business. "She kept calling me angel and stoking my cheek," Angie said about one Indian lady, a craftsman's wife whom she had met.

"And they'll do a better job thinking they are doing it for you," McNapp added. "Go ahead, be their angel and we'll buy our way to heaven."

They had taken about forty designs for bracelets and necklaces and McNapp had employed articians who had agreed to do about ten items each. "Four-hundred is about right for a first run," McNapp analyzed. But we need to test the market, see how these things sell before we commit ourselves to larger orders. I've got about a hundred pieces a friend gave me to sample. They're of inferior quality, but a trial run will help us iron out any problems. "I'll give you another thousand-dollars to handle it," he told Tom.

"When do I leave," Tom asked.

"Monday," McNapp replied. "I want you to drive this stuff to New Orleans and call Angie when you get there. Then I'll give you the name and address of our contact."

"Why don't you just give me that information now?" Tom asked.

"Believe me mate, it's smoother this way. It gives you less to worry about and keep up with. Also, I need to finalize the arrangements. Business is sometimes more complicated than it seems. There are certain people roaming around out there who just don't like me."

That night, Friday, McNapp threw Tom a going-away bash complete with the usual friends, prostitutes and cocaine. But this time McNapp introduced Tom to his guest as "my new business partner." The title didn't seem to fit Tom. He still dressed in tattered jeans, tee-shirts, Mexican sweaters and gauchos, and his hair stayed nearly shoulder-length. Also, he had recently cultivated his Emillo Zapata mustache until it drooped like a crooked crescent moon down the sides of chin. "You're going to have to clean up some, Tom," McNapp observed. "They don't like hippies at Customs. Just put on some decent clothes and cut your hair. Nothing personal you understand, just business."

The next afternoon Angie cut Tom's hair and shaved his moustache. He put on a new pair of tan slacks, a long-sleeved blue

Arrow button-down shirt and a pair of Earth shoes. He was a changed man.

"You look like you're right off the pages of GQ," I kidded.

"Not funny, John," he said scowling. "This is serious business. It's time to grow up a little."

McNapp had been cool to me since his business agreement with Tom. He grew cooler after I brought Lupita to Cuernervaca. Though he had told me to bring a guest if I wanted to entertain myself, he glared at her and said little after he returned from Taxco. His few remarks were sarcastic swipes at Mexican women. And his actions with the prostitutes bothered me. The guest room where Lupita and I were staying became their headquarters, and our bed became their office.

"Your friend," Lupita noticed. "He does not like me."

"I don't' know," I said, consoling her by the pool on Sunday afternoon. "He's just moody." But I was worried because he had an expression that I had never seen before, as if he knew a harmful secret that he was taking pleasure in keeping to himself. He knew his next move and I didn't. I was in check and his bishop had the angle on my lonely king in the black squares. But I hadn't wanted to play in the first place, and I wasn't sure about the rules.

That night at Harry's the situation escalated into a confusing predicament. McNapp talked convivially with Tom and Angie over our before-dinner margaritas, but stared at Lupita and me with his straight-lipped smile between words. It was so obvious I wondered why Tom and Angie didn't question him. I sensed then I was once again going to be the odd man out.

"Hey, John, let's go out and get some women. Tonight I'm paying," McNapp said casually.

Lupita lowered her eyes as if this baited insult was her fault. Hurt at this sudden move and eager to have the game end, I shook my head. I didn't have the strength to argue.

"What's the matter," he questioned. "You don't want to accept my hospitality anymore? Why the hell did ya bring that girl anyway. This is supposed to be business, not fun."

"You told me I could bring a guest," I reminded him. "If you don't want us here we'll leave." I felt my face flush with embarrassment as if I was a child being scolded. Strangely, I felt guilty of something I couldn't explain.

"Why don't you do that right now," McNapp snapped. You can go get your stuff and walk to the damn bus station. I don't want to see or hear from you again. Jesus, you make me sick. Just who the hell do you think you are?"

Stunned, Lupita and I returned to McNapp's, packed and in silence trudged to the bus station. I knew that my times with McNapp, Angie and Tom had ended. Angie and Tom had watched with timid resignation when Lupita and I left Harry's. They hadn't said a word. I guessed they were in too deep with McNapp to protest my treatment, and there just wasn't enough room for three in their alliance.

"He's not really your friend," Lupita said, trying to comfort me on the bus.

"I know," I reflected. "Worse, I think he's my enemy and I'm not sure why."

"Sure? What means sure?" Lupita asked.

"Seguro," I answered.

24

Angie was supposed to return to Mexico City after Tom left, but she didn't. I was afraid to call McNapp's, so I let it be. It wasn't my business anymore. Finally, I had the entire house to myself to read, wonder and maybe to start putting some of my own fractured legends on paper. School was starting soon and I wanted to take full advantage of the free time left.

Almost every night I took a crowded pesero cab to La Cavita, a dark bar located in a Zona Rosa basement. It was a pena, a bar where students and musicians congregated to discuss politics and sing folk songs. Instruments were provided and an assortment of guitars, bongo drums and tambourines sat in a corner awaiting use. The small crowd, usually no more than ten to fifteen people, knew each other. Some were close friends.

One wet night in early August I took Lupita with me. I had been in Mexico for nearly a year, so I thought I would make this a private anniversary party, my next to last one here. After next year I intended on moving on to someplace else, to Chile or Ecuador.

We drank and sang the despairing folk songs of resignation, the stories of so many Mexican lives. One student accompanied only by a guitar sang morosely:

> *Life is worth nothing,*
> *Nothing is what life's worth.*
> *It always begins with crying,*
> *And crying is how it ends.*
> *So that's why in this world*
> *Life is worth nothing.*

After eleven o'clock, several of the people proposed long-winded toasts that were political in nature and ended with some vague reference to "La Revolucion." Then a fat girl with a bandanna around her head read a long poem she had written titled "Por Che."

Then talk became critical of the current Mexican government. I listened carefully and tried to increase my Spanish fluency by inserting my own observations, those of a foreigner who loved liberty and understood their aspirations. Lupita made no comments. If someone asked her a question she responded "No se." She was uncomfortable and my talkative companions realized it.

"Why didn't you talk with those people," I asked her when we were back in her car.

"John, they are politicos," she calmly explained. "It is dangerous in Mexico to discuss politics. Haven't you heard of the Tlateloco massacre in 1968? The soldiers shot the students with machine guns and left them to die."

"Hell Lupita, those people were demonstrating against the government, not just talking in a bar."

"It does not matter, I know. I come from a family of politicians. Also, an election is coming soon. It is a bad time to discuss politics."

"I'm not worried," I protested. "Besides, I'm a foreigner, a Norte Americano."

"Still, I will not go with you to that bar again."

"Suit yourself."

Several nights later, after midnight, Tom called. "John, you've got to get out of Mexico," he implored in a frightened voice. "It's McNapp."

"What the hell," I moaned sleepily. "What about McNapp? Where are you?"

"This is serious John, just get out, and I can't tell you where I am. The phone may be bugged. Just get out, quick."

"At least tell me the problem. If I'm going to have to leave my job it doesn't matter. Anyway, this is Mexico. I don't think they know how to bug phones down here."

"OK," Tom agreed solemnly. "There was a lot of turquoise in that jewelry. It didn't look right. Some of it looked like boulders hanging by silver threads. I got suspicious and busted a piece with a hammer. The turquoise was nothing but hard plastic. There was heroin inside, pure looking stuff. John, I bet that haul was worth over a hundred grand on the street. I've been used for a goddamn mule!" Tom knew he had invested in death, not life. Perhaps he still had time to escape this explosive mine and sink back into the safety of the mountains.

"Shit Tom, what are you going to do? Why don't you turn that stuff over to the cops?"

"You kiddin, they'd arrest me. What would I do, tell them all about McNapp? And besides, no telling who he knows up here. I just don't know about this thing. I'm going to dump this stuff and disappear. And then he's going to come looking for you! I figure you've got about a week. When he doesn't hear from me or his contact, he's going to get real anxious." The connection was fading and the line began to sound like popcorn popping.

"OK" I agreed, pressing my ear against the receiver as if the closeness would improve the sound. "I'll leave as soon as I can. Get in touch with me back in the States."

"No," he replied. That's too dangerous. I tell you I'm gonna disappear. It's the best way. Let me speak with Angie."

"She's not here, Tom," I shouted into the mouthpiece. "She hasn't come back from McNapp's."

"What, I can barely hear you."

"She's with McNapp!"

"Damn, John, you've got to warn her. Get her out of there. McNapp's obviously using her to keep me in line. She's his security. No telling what'll happen to her now. Please John, do it for me. Can you hear me?"

"Yes," I screamed. "But you could do it. Just get the stuff to his contact and then return and sneak off with Angie. You didn't know, you're not responsible."

"No. Then we would be in too deep. We could never escape. This is the only way. John, you've got to do this. Please try. You know how much I love her."

"OK, I'll try," I said. "If I succeed I'll leave a message at the AAA office in Houston. You can call in and find out."

There was a crackling tension as we both searched out separate mental maps. There would be a long time, maybe a forever of suspense, of not knowing. There would be a long time all along the watchtower seeing nothing. The wildcat had growled.

"Adios, Bro," Tom said.

"Adios," I replied.

The next morning I took a Flecha Orja to Cuernervaca. I had no other choice. After putting so much energy into the heroic, I had little to show for it except a few survival mountain climbs, a wounded escape from the federales and a trail of dubious sexual conquests. I felt strangely reluctant, but I had promised Tom I would try and warn Angie. Besides, I was partially responsible for this mess. I was one of the cooks who had spiced this poison stew. I, too, had learned what McNapp was and how he was and every addition to the recipe had just sweetened my appetite while I complimented the master chef. He had led me to the table and I had eaten, but now it was time to vomit.

I arrived at noon. I knew that I had no chance of getting past McNapp's gate. My only hope was to isolate her at Harry's during happy hour. Until then, I concealed myself in the familiar back streets away from the Zocalo. I thought about hiding in one of the peasant cantinas, but the smell of the leftover night sawdust kept me beyond those swinging doors. Besides, those were not my people. Once an hour, hoping to catch Angie walking to town, I took a cab past McNapp's gate. But I knew this tactic was futile. Angie spoke only a few words of Spanish and didn't enjoy being on her own. It was Harry's or nothing.

I hadn't solved the problem of how not to be seen. I couldn't be somebody's Corporal. My best plan was to sit at the rear of the restaurant section at the table closest to the Damas restroom. McNapp and his group always sat in the front facing the Zocalo. To see me they would have to walk around the bar towards the restroom. But, I could see them if I leaned around the edge of the bar. Contacting Angie would be simple. She had the smallest bladder I knew. She would excuse herself before she ordered her second drink.

I got there at four o'clock. Fortunately, I didn't recognize the waiters. They wouldn't accidentally bring me to McNapp's attention. During the next hour I ordered three shots of tequila to steady my nerves. After the last one I chuckled to myself about the possibilities. Old Sarte never had a chance like this. All he did was get sick. Here I am, facing death at the hands of an Australian mafia man near the ladies room in a Mexican bar. But I was prepared. I had even brought my machete, a dull rusty thing I had bought at the thieves market for forty pesos. It was funny all right, but who would laugh with me if I got caught. Would they talk about it at my high school reunion?

McNapp's cuadrilla arrived at five o'clock. He was with Angie and three of his friends, including the Colonel. Another one I recognized as Antonio, the yes man who had been present at all the parties. He had his arm around Angie and they were laughing. They were high. Even from a distance I noticed Angie's eyes, wide like an owl's, but shadowed with darkness that sunk into her cheeks. After they ordered their first drinks, Antonio leaned over and kissed her, a sloppy Latino public kiss. She put her head against his shoulder and ran her long fingers up and down his arms as if she were stoking a pet. The others paid no attention. McNapp sat smoking and looking out towards the Zocalo while he talked to the Colonel. The smoke rings formed warped halos about his head while he talked and tapped his fingers on his whiskey. He reached over with his free arm and poured the Colonel a drink, but the old man didn't touch it. He just adjusted his dark glasses and crossed his arms.

It was then I decided Angie wasn't worth it. I knew I couldn't make her realize this thing had gone beyond self. Angie, spoiled Jewish American Princess that she was, had the clearest myopia of any of us. She was oblivious to consequences for herself as well as other people. She wasn't going to leave. She was a fallen angel and hell was the voluntary abode of those soiled beings. I would send Tom the message and hope he understood. Anyway, this was over. I had kept my promise to Tom. I had tried.

I turned my back to the bar and pulled up the collar of my new leather jacket. Suddenly, as if it were warning me, I felt the machete point stick through the rotten sheath and prick my side. But, she didn't recognize me. I'm not so sure she could have even if we were face to face. She stumbled slightly going into the bathroom and let out a girlish giggle. She was out of it, her brain swirling in a whirlpool of drugs and booze, the jacuzzi of the seventies and the times to come.

Fortunately, they left after the second drink. I gave them a ten minute head start, paid my bill and walked out of happy hour. I glanced at Cortez's old house one last time and walked slowly to the bus station. It was time to leave.

25

The old Aztec calendar, the one illustrated on the massive Sun Stone in the Museum of Anthropology, shows eighteen months of twenty days each. Five days were left to explain. These were called "nemontemtim," or the "lifeless days," days between time. The Aztecs loaded these days with evil portent, men stepped carefully and women stayed inside, avoiding these holidays of the soul. I knew I was living in those days. I hated to leave Mexico, my adopted country, and return to the life insurance salesmen life of the United States of America. My life there was dead. I had no reason to return. But again, I had no choice. Sooner or later, probably sooner, McNapp would come after me. That was a sure thing. Seguro.

I resigned my teaching position, sold our household goods to some new teachers from Iowa, had my Capri repaired by a mechanic who used stolen parts and packed Tom's mask collection for shipment to his sister's home in Montgomery. I included my conquistador mask. Tom would understand. But its bearded face with its leering grin seemed to be saying "Fool, fool, who were you to try and create me again. I am a legend. I lived in the world I made. And You?" I shoved the mask to the bottom of the crate and covered it with paper from by bullfight magazines. I was through with history for a while.

On the last lifeless night, the night before I left Mexico, I went to La Cavita. It was after ten o'clock when I arrived and I was surprised that none of my Mexican friends were there already drinking and singing. It was quiet, too quiet. Normally, the waiters bustled with pleasant energy, but tonight they were nervous and slow, their eyes darting like lizard tongues around the bar.

There were only four other patrons: a dark-skinned ageless woman smoking a cigarette in a holder and three young men seated by a long table at the back of the bar. I ordered a Cerveza Barril and began drinking and waiting for the festivities to start. Then the three men rose and headed for the stairs leading up to the bar's only door. Suddenly, as I lifted the mug to my lips, one of the men reached under my arm pits and cupped his hands around the back of my neck. My mug crashed to the table and before I could resist another of them clubbed me on top of the head with the butt of a .38 pistol. He didn't knock me unconscious. He had aimed too high. "What the fuck," I yelled, twisting my right elbow and powering it into the wrestler's cheek. I knocked him off, but the other two assailants seized me while two other men from outside rushed down the stairs. One of them kicked me in the stomach and I crumpled to the floor under a hailstorm of blows.

They dragged me up the stairs and out of the door into the slippery streets of the Zona Rosa where my strength returned as I caught my breath. I felt no pain. I sensed I was fighting against death. Nobody gets out of here alive was the rule about disappearances in Mexico. And these men weren't wearing uniforms: they could be guerillas kidnapping me for ransom, or worse, McNapp's men.

"Ayuga me, Ayuga me," I yelled in Spanish, and then, "Help me, Help me," in English as I tried to swirl and kick away from this nightmare. A crowd had formed in the street and I could see their faces pass in a blur. One of the kidnappers was standing a few feet away from the struggle waving something in his hand back and forth at the crowd. "Why don't they help me?" I wondered. "Why doesn't someone help me?" While I was spinning like a wobbly top I spied a woman in a mink stole. She crossed her arms and pulled the stole tighter to her body with her fingers. She appeared bored. I fixed my gaze on her.

The men were trying to force me into a white Rambler Ambassador but with little success. Then I felt the cold steel of the .38 barrel against my temple. "Johnny, get in the car," I heard in English. The threatened death sentence to the brain convinced me to obey. Maybe I would have a chance to escape.

The Rambler swerved off the side streets and into the Reforma traffic. The kidnappers were silent. I only heard labored breaths. After a ten minute eternity the car turned onto Insurgentes. The .38 was no longer pointed at my head so I relaxed and, as I hoped, so did the two men holding me. I was seated between them in the back seat and the two other men were in the front. Between these men was a console with an open space separating the front seats. This space was wide enough for me to get my foot through. I knew this might be my only chance. If I just got out of the car I could escape on foot. I would worry about the rest later. The captors still gripped my arms tightly but my legs were free. My chance came when the driver turned left off Insurgentes. I kicked his right arm as hard as I could with my left foot. The car bounced over the curb and caremed off a street lamp pole, hitting it with the left front fender. I had hoped for a head-on collision. I lunged for the left back door, away from the triggerman, but the collision wasn't enough to knock the men out. I didn't even get the door open before I felt a fist in my balls. I collapsed on the seat with the now-familiar gun stuck under my chin. My escape attempt was over.

"No, Johnny. Policia," the man to my left said calmly in English. He pushed me back against the seat and motioned for his partner to put the gun away. Then he showed me his badge and identification. "It is OK Johnny," he continued. "I am a detective. My name is Roberto. I am your friend."

"Thank God, I thought you were guerillas," I stuttered. That warm feeling that things were OK, that I wasn't guilty, ran though me like cognac on a cold night. Maybe I wouldn't be found dead in a ditch, my body food for peasant pigs. This detective was so calm, even friendly. Maybe everything would be alright. But fears welled up quickly. These were the Mexican secret police! "What did I do?" I wailed. "Where are you taking me?"

"Just relax, Johnny. Everything will be OK," Roberto repeated, patting my leg like a friendly uncle. "You are here because there is something we need to know, but first we eat. We waited a long time for you. We are hungry. Do you want something to eat?"

"No," I replied weakly. Blood dripped on my white sweater from the top of my head. I could feel it slipping through my hair like trickles of sweat on a hot day.

The driver pulled over and went into a small tacoria. I could smell the broiling meat through the open car window. Robert pulled out a handkerchief and wiped the blood off of my face. "Keep this," he said, handing it to me. "What is wrong? You don't like Mexican food?" he asked.

"I do, yes I do," I replied apologetically, wiping the blood from my forehead.

"I thought you did. You had so many Mexican friends. Do you like Mexican girls?"

"Yes, very much." Somehow I thought this was a test of allegiance, and if I showed my love for his country and his people I could pass. "I have had many Mexican girlfriends."

"Yes, we know."

Roberto and the other men ate their tacos in the car while we continued to slither like a moccasin through streets as dark as a night river. I was always cognizant of the location, my mind locking in on points of the city like a compass reading. At one point we passed by the old Aztec aqueduct near the Avenida Chapultepec. Then, we slid into the Calle de los Ninos Periditos. The street lights still illuminated the caskets in the store windows, the K-Marts for the dead. I didn't see myself in one. That would be a luxury. I knew if I died this night I would be found in a barranca outside town, a refuse covered mummy with a scream on my face and no one would light candles around my body or bring me a feast on the Day of the Dead.

"Tu es muy fuente," one of my captors in the front seat commented while he turned to me flexing his bicep.

"He said you are very strong because you fight hard," Roberto translated, even though he knew I understood.

"I know. I speak Spanish."

"Yes, I know you do," Roberto responded. "But I think it is best that we speak in English. You need to understand everything. You have rights, no? Your police taught me that when I worked for them."

"You said you needed to know something," I said, wiping off more blood, this time from my cheek. "How can I help you?" I felt as dependent as a spoiled child on Roberto. I would've told him anything, even spilled my guts about McNapp if he had asked. I would've taken the chance that he didn't work for him.

"Alto aqui," Roberto commanded the driver. He pulled up by a bus maintenance building. I knew the place: one block north of the Avenida Chapultepec and some distance west of Insurgentes.

"Johnny, why did you rape that girl? The one from La Cavita. You know, Senorita Alvarez." He seemed to struggle for the name, as if he were searching a phone book for verification. "You did it this way and this way," Roberto said, pointing to his front and back. "And then you tried to kill her." His tone didn't change. It was almost patronizing, as if a father was scolding his favorite child.

"No," I gasped. "I didn't. I swear. I don't know what you're talking about. I'm innocent. You've got to believe me," I begged.

Roberto put his hand on my shoulder and peered into my face.

A lone passing car lit up his dark marble eyes. "Johnny, if she says that it was you, you will stay in prison all of your life." I learned then that helpless fear is like being sucked up by a giant vacuum cleaner: first, a rush; then, a loss of breath; and finally, terror's emptiness.

Two other men approached the car from the parking area and opened the back door by the driver's side. Roberto gently led me out of the car by pulling slightly on my left arm. Then one of the men placed a pistol in the small of my back while they guided me like a stumbling drunk to the bathroom in the depot. Roberto stayed outside guarding the door. The men stripped me from the waist down and tied my hands behind my back with leather thongs. Then the gunman pushed my head in the toilet until I choked on the fresh urine. He yanked me up by the hair and stuck the gun into my mouth. I heard the hammer click when he pulled the trigger. "Go ahead," I thought. "Spare me a Mexican prison. I don't want my mother to die of worry or my friends to get into trouble if I talk. And I know I can't take the pain of prison. If they don't do it now, I'll find a way to do it myself. I'll hang myself with sheets." I tried to remember how to tie a handman's knot. I hadn't tied one since I was a Cub Scout testing for my Lion's badge. The hammer clicked three more times, a Mexican Roulette game. Then they untied me, ordered me to put on my pants and dragged me like a matinee movie rustler cut down from a rope back to the Rambler. And I feared this was just the early show with the main feature still to come.

"Cigarette," Roberto offered. "They are Marlboros." He lit up, inhaled deeply and exhaled out the window. He was quiet and appeared distracted, as if pondering a problem.

"No thank you," I answered calmly as if I had just returned from a vacation. "I don't smoke."

"Too bad, he reflected. "Sometimes it helps you to think about things."

We drove again into the back streets. I didn't feel any pain from my head but my terror was howling like a banshee. I prayed silently promising I would become a Baptist minister, preaching to the rich and feeding the poor, if God would only deliver me from this agony.

"You know your friends at La Cavita, Johnny?" Roberto said. "You will not see them again."

I was silent.

"What we need to know is where you will go if we let you free?"

My terror lessened. Perhaps I had some control. I knew I had to give some right answers. My hope began to fill like a homemade down pillow. "I would leave for the United States in a few days," I answered calmly, the stinging pain of the leather still burning my wrist.

"Would you go to the embassy before you left?" Roberto beat the bottom of a new cigarette pack, loosening its contents.

"No," I faked a laugh. "I never go to the embassy for anything. But could you tell me about my friends?

"Who," Roberto asked with surprise. He thought he had made himself clear about my friends.

"Guadelope Carranza Solice, Lupita, my girlfriend," I answered slowly and clearly.

"I do not know that name."

"She's the niece of Senor Munoz Leydo, the president of PRI," I informed him. "She comes with me to La Cavita. I have a letter in my wallet from him."

I didn't want to push him, challenge his sense of importance, his machismo. But if he thought this was a trick pass with a bad bull, I was covered.

But he didn't ask. Perhaps he was smart enough to figure out I would never attempt such a bluff. There was to much to lose. Now it was his bull.

Roberto turned to the side window, lit another cigarette and smoked for a few minutes. "You want a cerveza Johnny?" he asked as we stopped at a tenienda.

"Yes, I'll have a Bohemia."

Roberto and two of his partners left the car and went up to the open facade. They stood and talked for several minutes after they bought the beer. The driver stayed in the car and kept a lazy eye on me. When they returned, Roberto handed me the cold Bohemia and I drank it down like a guilty, alcoholic priest gulping sacramental wine.

"Johnny, we are going to see the girl," Roberto reported. "If she says that it was you, you go to jail. If she says no, you will go home to the United States, OK?"

Less than five minutes later the Rambler turned into an ink-dark alley. From the darkness a stout young woman emerged by the right rear window. Roberto got out of the car and spoke to a man accompanying the woman. He was the fifth involved in my kidnapping, the one showing the crowd what must have been his badge.

"Johnny," Roberto commanded. "Put your face to the window." The man on my right placed a flashlight under my chin as I leaned over him. Through the open window, the night air smelled like sour milk. The woman leaned to within three inches of my face. Her face was pocked like the weather-chiselled remains of some Aztec god's visage. "No! El no estaba alli!," she said. *HE WAS NOT THERE.*

"Johnny, she said it was not you," Roberto said matter-of-factly as he closed the car door. "We made a mistake. You can go. But first we need to take you to the hospital. You are hurt. This must have happened when you were fighting with us. But you will tell the doctor that you hurt your head playing soccer, OK?"

"OK," I agreed.

Ten minutes later I was at the Seguro Sociale clinic near the intersection of Chapultepec and Ninos Periditos. I didn't think that Roberto and his friends knew that I knew where I was. The entire night had been designed to confuse me where I couldn't trace my steps, or I couldn't escape. But I always knew. Like a war veteran, I knew even in darkness. The streets were drawn in my consciousness with a cartographer's accuracy. I knew where I would live or die.

Roberto presented me to two young interns in green smocks. He flashed them his badge and no words passed. As they led me in to a treatment room they shut the door in Roberto's face. He knocked, but one of the interns cracked the door and said a few quick words in Spanish I didn't understand. "It's fine mister," one said, softly closing the door. "Come."

I was led to a cot and stitches were put in my head. It hurt like hell because there was no anesthesia. The clinic had run out of its monthly allowance. While they were working the interns talked to me. "They bring many people in here," one said. "We have a book. Put your name in the book. If your people come to look for you, we have your name. The policia do not know of this book." I signed the book: my name, Alabama address and my mother's name. I felt like a vegetable can in the garbage and once again I was afraid I would be thrown out with the night's waste.

"You want to leave now," one of the interns asked after they had finished the repairs.

"Not really," I answered. I would try and stall the possible. Maybe this was it. This stale white room with light as pale as hangover piss would be my final view, the photograph I would take with me into eternity.

An intern brought me a thick textbook and turned to a middle page. "You can translate this?" he asked. I read slowly, attempting to pronounce the hodge-podge of medical terms. "No," he interrupted, "read the verbs."

I read through several pages of the text. It concerned heart surgery. When I finished, the interns apologized for having to return me to Roberto and the others.

Next, they drove me to a police station and led me to a small, dark room where I was seated on a long hardwood bench resembling a church pew. Against the wall was a black metal desk with a rotund officer sitting behind it scribbling notes in a ledger. He had the same stone look of the automobile customs official at the border. Roberto spoke with him for a few minutes and then returned to me. "Johnny," he said. "There are papers for you to sign. Come and read them."

I stepped up to the desk, my hollow heart pounding like the inside of a Ludwig bass drum in a Led Zepplin concert. The fat officer shoved a typed document in front of me. I was afraid I was signing a confession condemning me to prison. If I refused to sign it, a cattle prod would light up my balls like Ben Franklin's kite, or worse, there would be no more light at all. I only saw it for about a minute, but the Spanish words for "not responsible" and "leave Mexico" were there several times.

"This says that you were hurt on the head playing football," Roberto translated. "And that you will leave Mexico in thirty days. You Agree?"

"I do," I said, quickly consummating a marriage with survival as I signed the papers. There were ten copies.

Roberto led me outside to the street. A solitary street lamp's light fluttered beside the police station's front door. "Johnny," he said, shaking his head from side to side. "We are sorry. You understand. You will leave Mexico in thirty days?"

"I will," I said.

"Good," he said. "Now, you want to go have some girls with us tonight. I know a good place."

"No," I answered. "I'm tired. It's been a long night."

Roberto waved as I walked away toward the Avenita Chapultepec. I returned his farewell, but when I turned the corner I ran. When I reached Chapultepec, only three blocks away, I hailed a taxi. "Calle Jimenez y Muor, numero veinte ocho," I directed the driver as I flopped inside. He hesitated an instant before he pulled away. My white sweater was soaked with blood, I had a bandage on the top of my head and I stunk. For the first time, I could feel in my jeans the softness of the night's fear.

26

It was three in the morning when the taxi driver dropped me off. I calmly unlocked the gate and numbly strolled down the driveway, my legs disappearing beneath me. Inside Tom's stereo was softly humming:

> It's been a long time comin;
> It's going to be a long time gone.
> But you know the darkest hour is always, always,
> Just before the dawn.

But I wasn't interested in music anymore. I climbed the stairs without switching on the lights. I wanted darkness, not the dim scenes of the private terror I had just experienced. My salvation had come out of the night: *NO ESTABA ALLI*. Whatever the situation, those words had saved me: the definition of a nowhere man in a nowhere place. I was not there, but I always would be.

I stood in the shower and scrubbed myself until the gas ran out and the water turned cold. I patted myself dry with a fluffy towel, the kind I loved so much when I was little, wrapped it around me and walked into Tom's bedroom, only a few steps away.

"I've been waiting for you." Her legs swung slowly from the hammock in Tom's old room and her gray outline smudged the bedroom wall where the mask had hung. "We have to leave."

"I know. The secret police picked me up tonight. I think they would have killed me but I made them nervous about who I knew. I'm afraid they'll come back."

"You're right," Angie said, lighting up a joint. "I heard McNapp talking to somebody on the phone. I didn't understand much, just,

John, Norteamericano and policia, but that was enough. He had bragged about how some policemen still owed him for favors, and it looks like you were one of them. The last few days he began to lose his temper. He was nervous about Tom. He slapped me around yesterday. He kept saying, where's Tom, where's Tom you hippie bitch." She took a long hit and held it in her lungs. Her breasts deflated slowly as she released.

"Did you give him any suggestions?" A trace of the old sarcasm born out of mistrust slid from my tongue.

"No," she answered, ignoring it. "I told him Tom's friends were out west around Seattle and that he'd probably go out there instead of Montgomery. But I don't think he believed me. I know he didn't. And I told him there were no more hippies." She crushed the half-smoked joint against the bed's brass rail and let it drop to the floor.

"I guess you know the jewelry was loaded," I said.

"Yes, I figured out that much. But I didn't care. Jesus, I mean look at me. I love the stuff. I've been doing all of it since we went to McNapp's. I've even been shooting it the last couple of weeks. It cleans you out you know, makes you sweat spiritually, a sort of enema for the soul."

"Then why did you leave," I asked. "You had it all, drugs, money, goodlooking men, all free." I expected a flush, a hot response. But she sensed my weak attempts at an emotional battle, my own reflective surrender.

"I don't know why," she answered. "Maybe instinct just took over. Or maybe a little voice whispered in my head 'get out.' Or maybe I just loved you and Tom too much. I should have left earlier, when you came for me. But I was just so screwed up."

"You knew?" I asked.

"Yes, I did."

She slid out of the hammock and drifted toward me like a child's early morning ghost. "Hold me," she cooed, this time without Carlota's accompaniment. I circled her naked, shivering body with my arms, sensing her beads of moisture despite the cool night air.

I had dreamed this, imagined this passion born of desperation and futility. I cradled Angie and laid her on Tom's bed, where we slept and made love to our imaginations, to the images of ourselves we had brought to Mexico.

Seven o'clock brought fear for breakfast. The realities returned. We had to leave immediately. We took only one bag each. I had already shipped most of my belongings and Angie had left most of hers at McNapp's. By nine we were on the road to San Miguel, the same road Tom and I had travelled a year ago on our way to Mexico City. Leaving the Valley of Mexico, we climbed into the encircling mountains. I veered onto the road's shoulder beside a peasant who was heading toward some Mexico City market, his donkey loaded with pots and pans. The wares rattled as the donkey came to a halt and the man gave me a cursory glance. Then, they turned and continued on their way. Despite the early morning hour, I fished two Bohemias out of the cooler and walked with Angie to the edging that separated the shoulder from the cliff.

"You know," I said, looking out over the tops of the grey-clouded buildings of Mexico City. "I've always wanted to have a good feeling about things when they ended. I'm trying to get that feeling now."

"You better take what you can get," Angie said.

"I know," I replied. "I'm trying to do that now."

We killed the beers in silence, returned to the car and continued north. I felt this was the safest escape route. If he was after us, McNapp would be watching the airport and bus terminals and he had not known us when my car was running. We could disappear into the desert wasteland of the north and hide among the armadillos, rocks and industrial smog, and then choose our border crossing. We could lose ourselves.

By three we were in San Miguel. We checked into the San Francisco Hotel and went immediately to the restaurant, which was furnished with Spanish Colonial antiques and surrounded by an indoor garden. Here, I felt fresh and safe. We didn't talk over the first bottle of wine, just drifted around our own spaces. We were together but apart and, like Venus and Mars, in the same system on the edge of the Milky Way but revolving in different orbits.

"So where are you going after we get there, that is," she asked.

"I haven't thought about it yet," I answered. "I never intended to leave. I won't make any plans for a while. It's too dangerous. I need to go home and check on my mother. Then maybe I'll be a college professor, a writer or a mountaineer. At any rate I'll go somewhere else. What about you?"

"I'm going to stay with my father," she answered quickly. "He owns stables and horses up in Minnesota. I can ride every day until I'm too tired to think about anything. Just ride and ride and ride until I ride off the end of the earth."

"My father was a Navy man," I motioned to the waiter for another bottle of wine. "He served in the South Pacific. I have pictures of him with kangaroos and women with saggy tits. He didn't marry until he was forty-seven, and then I'm not so sure what he wanted to find, a respite maybe, from what he didn't find. Maybe I'm just a chip off the old block. Maybe that's what it's all about: running into dead ends, and then turning around and looking for shortcuts and then becoming lost again. And what about the stuff, the smack? Do you think you're OK?"

"I think so, but I've got to get away from it. You see, it makes me feel immortal, takes me outside of time, controls my dreams. Of course, if I get sick for it, I'll go for treatment. Some nice comfortable private hospital where everything is sterile and secret. My father will take care of it. He's taken care of me before. He got me an abortion when I got pregnant by a black professor at college. From him I don't get lectures, just action. The future is always starting over."

"So like a cat you've got nine lives," I observed.

"No, just one," she responded.

"And what about Tom?" I asked.

"He's still in my life," she answered. "You see my life is like a mansion with many rooms and he's tucked away in one now, just waiting for me to wake him up again."

"And when will that be," I asked.

"When I've visited all of the other rooms," she answered, swallowing her last glass of wine. "You have a room too, but it's small, not as spacious as Tom's and it's not as well-lighted. I tried to throw you out of it but you refused to leave."

"And McNapp and his group," I asked.

"They're there too," she answered, "hidden in the closets and dark corners."

That night we slept apart.

We left before daylight. The streets were cool and damp from a late-night rain and this world was still. On the way out I circled the Zocalo and stopped in front of the cathedral. I had always seen these places mainly from the outside. Now, I wanted to see inside, to see if I could sense their mystery. Angie didn't want to go so I pushed open the heavy wooden door and faced the dark interior alone. It took a few moments for my eyes to adjust, but then I saw no one else was here. Three statues of saints, like those in Sam's house, stood against each wall, but it was too dark to see anything but the outlines of the ornamentation in the loft. Candles burned in front of the alter. Someone must have been here before me. Now, at last, I wanted to make love to Angie, right here in front of God's alter. We could create an apocalypse of our recent past, erase it from memory and bury it in the candles' paraffin to serve as penitence for others, our sacrifice.

I felt as if I should pray but I didn't know what about, so I turned and softly closed the door as if trying not to disturb the sleeping statues.

27

You see it's all clear,
You were meant to be here,
From the beginning...
                    —Emerson, Lake and Palmer

We didn't head straight for the border. Instead, I took us on a detour through Guanajuato. I had to see the mummies, the ones that had so fascinated the Colonel. I wanted to see if they meant the same thing to me as they did him.

They were displayed in a modern air-conditioned museum just outside this lovely colonial town, the big sister to San Miguel. It no longer appeared strange to me, this juxtapositioning of the beautiful and the grotesque. It was just Mexico. As usual, street vendors swarmed around the door. I bought a leather belt, my last souvenir, from a reputable looking stall. On its buckle was a brass eagle surrounded by stars. I paid the man's asking price because I didn't feel like bargaining anymore or having to exchange pesos into dollars on the other side. I wanted to leave broke.

Inside, I went looking for the woman with the baby, the dried up madonna about whom the Colonel had spoken. She was half-way down the row of glass cases. Unlike, the other mummies whose faces stared straight ahead or were twisted to the side, the madonna's face was thrown up towards heaven as if she were asking God for a favor, or thanking him for one. The tattered baby was still curled in her ripped belly, the umbilical cord twisted around it like a bird's nest of fishing line.

"Do you think it knew anything, I mean, about what happened?" Angie asked.

"You mean did it suffer terror and confusion? I don't think so. I think it just disappeared back where it came from, another eternity. It never knew the difference."

Would you rather be that baby or that old woman Tom told me about who died in the street covered with chicklets and surrounded by candles?"

"I'll take the chicklets. And especially the candles," I answered.

By early afternoon we were on Highway 85. Again, I passed through Saltillo and Monterray. Timelessly, the same children were hawking armadillos by the roadside on the high desert, holding them up by tails, their heads hanging harmlessly towards the sand.

"The Indians believe they carry leprosy," I said.

"Maybe that's why they want to sell them to us," Angie replied.

We arrived in Nuevo Laredo that night, passing through the shadowy flatness where the freak carnival had stood. Now I understood the unexplained fear that I had experienced last year when I returned to the hotel. People didn't come here for fantasy. They were experiencing reality for a price, one they thought they could control. We were all punching midgets.

It was too late to clear customs so we spent the night at the Ramada Inn. I could see we were close to the States because the glasses and the toilet seat in the room were wrapped in paper and the green shag carpet looked like suburban grass that needed mowing. There was a room service menu by the phone. It had all the fancy dishes, including lobster, but I wasn't hungry and neither was Angie. She went downstairs to the pool and I ordered a fish sandwich just to get me through the night.

From the balcony I could see the lights from Los Estados Unitos, the tall buildings' shadows lighter against a black sky leading to eternity. Before I had come to Mexico, I wanted to leave behind my history. I had failed. I had been chasing old myths when I needed new ones, so there was going to be a coming home whether

I accepted it or not, a reckoning in my own territory. What scared me was McNapp might know it. I knew I would look over my left shoulder into dark corners, side streets and vacant rooms expecting to see him on the edge of my vision. Or I might see Tom, his finger motioning me again in a direction he didn't understand himself, and not caring if I followed him into dead times.

Already, Angie was talking with another man, one who looked familiar another Latin with a basket full of dark, curly hair and gold medallions glittering like distress signals from his chest. Before long, Angie was lightly touching his arm to make her points and he was casting furtive glimpses at her breast while he flipped the hair off her shoulders. They left within the hour, around nine.

Behind me was Mexico. I thought about the old Mexicans, the ones who had met Cortez and how they had to construct their lives over, adapt to change, accept the inevitable, but somehow twist their lives toward the sun within the shadows of their past. I hadn't done as well. I had attempted to rebuild on the shifting sands of illusions and not on the rocky foundations of my past, however broken.

North, in front of me was home. Wounded and beaten, ole David Bragg's kin had hauled him there in a wagon over wet, bloody roads. That trip over the hills of Tennessee and North Alabama and into Greene County had certainly taken longer than any automobile rush would take, but I still felt that in many ways my trip had already covered more territory. I knew I had changed and was still changing, but I wasn't sure how. I did know that Evelyn was now only a kindergarten memory, Cortez a museum piece and my father dead.

At three, I was awakened from a troubled sleep by a banging at the door. When I opened it Angie tumbled inside against my feet. Her one-piece bathing suit was gone and she wore a man's tee shirt with *Dallas Cowboys 66* and a pair of soiled, silk underwear. Her mouth formed a crooked oval, like the entrance to a cave, her hair stuck to her neck with vomit and fresh needle marks dotted her left arm like the scabies we had once cured. When I put her in bed, I found our room key pinned to the back of the jersey.

I knew it was brutal, but I had to leave her. This was still Mexico and I would be blamed either for her drugs or her death. Brutal? Yes, but at least something I could live with rather than die. Here, you are responsible for the tragedies you find, your brother or sister's appointed keeper. She had found me in her house, but I was leaving the room because she had found someone else in one of the dark corners who would also destroy me.

My goods were already in the car. I only paused when I reached inside the table drawer to grab my fistful of pesos and found a neatly folded square of paper tucked away in the right corner. A poem:

> *I go among the thieves and perverts*
> *and the junkies of streetlight distraction*
> *until finally they recognize my approach.*
> *I get the same taste in my mouth*
> *and their bitter weakness.*
> *I am a Madman and a Poet.*
> *I have been given the anger and the terror,*
> *the one I hold tightly in my left hand*
> *and keep the other from running away.*
> *Take my sin with a woman*
> *and now she is wicked,*
> *and she loved me in her sleep*
> *and trembled, so her breath fell away*
> *like the wind takes her dress off the night.*

> *—Morgan*

Shotgun, Squid, McNapp and now Morgan? Who was Morgan? Another incomplete name, incomplete life. Perhaps. But it was my life so far and Angie was a piece of it. I walked back and broke the crusted hair, smoothing it on the pillow. Angie. I thought how close I had come to heeding the siren call of this dark angel. I pulled her driver's license from her purse and placed it on the table by the bed.

Three blocks from the Ramada I stopped at a Pemex gas station and called room service. I told the bored, mechanical voice that the daughter of a wealthy and influential American was very ill in room 33 and needed an ambulance, immediately. I prayed for her to live.

I drove slowly through the deserted streets past where the sidewalk jockey had sped from his tormentors and to the bridge over the Rio Bravo. I parked in the lot next to Mexican Customs and walked to the middle. My walk disturbed some birds, pigeons or crows, and I watched them soar towards the moon with dark flaps of their numberless wings.

The Mexican guards were leaning against the bridge rails and smoking. They didn't stop me for a documents check or a search. I would be the Norte Americanos' problem in a few hours. Besides, hundreds of Mexican workers were already milling around waiting to cross over to their American jobs. Some squatted on their haunches smoking cigarettes and drinking coffee heated on a two-burner Coleman stove. "You, hombre," one called to me. "Coffee Mexicana?" I walked over and took the full plastic cup he offered. "Gracias," I said.

"You like Mexico, hombre?"

"Si, I like Mexico."

"You like Mexican women?"

"Si, I like Mexican women."

"Good, Good." Satisfied, he turned back to his friends.

Sipping the hot, black coffee, I turned toward the United States of America and sensed I had been riding on midnight, sampling life's experiences on the edge of a new day and yet beginning again. I would cross the border alone. Tom was somewhere over there, in hiding, perhaps in New Orleans, or perhaps Atlanta, or San Francisco, or Miami, or Boston, or Birmingham, or maybe no place. Just like me.

—END—